"A food competition? I'd lose without a doubt, Will."

"I wouldn't be so sure," he replied. "Wasn't it you who told me the owner has confidence in her food?"

"It would certainly allow the town to form their own opinions about my food." Kara slumped. "But if it goes badly, it could be the nail in my café's coffin."

"Not going to happen. I've eaten your crepes." Will took both of her hands. "And trust me, darlin', there's no way you'll lose."

She smelled amazing. Like vanilla. Will took a deep breath. "I promise you won't regret taking this chance."

"I won't, because only with great risk—" Kara gave him a quick kiss on his cheek "—comes great reward." She smiled at him.

If he gazed long enough into the liquid blue pool of her eyes, Will believed he might drown. But for once, he didn't care…

Lisa Carter and her family make their home in North Carolina. In addition to her Love Inspired novels, she writes romantic suspense. When she isn't writing, Lisa enjoys traveling to romantic locales, teaching writing workshops and researching her next exotic adventure. She has strong opinions on barbecue and ACC basketball. She loves to hear from readers. Connect with Lisa at lisacarterauthor.com.

Books by Lisa Carter

Love Inspired

Visit the Author Profile page at Harlequin.com.

A Chance for the Newcomer

Lisa Carter

LOVE INSPIRED

INSPIRATIONAL ROMANCE

LOVE INSPIRED®
INSPIRATIONAL ROMANCE

Recycling programs
for this product may
not exist in your area.

ISBN-13: 978-1-335-48893-0

A Chance for the Newcomer

This edition published by arrangement with Harlequin Books S.A.

For questions and comments about the quality of this book, please contact us at CustomerService@Harlequin.com.

Love Inspired
22 Adelaide St. West, 40th Floor
Toronto, Ontario M5H 4E3, Canada
www.Harlequin.com

Printed in U.S.A.

Brethren, I count not myself to have
apprehended: but this one thing I do,
forgetting those things which are behind, and
reaching forth unto those things which are
before, I press toward the mark for the prize of
the high calling of God in Christ Jesus.
—*Philippians* 3:13–14

Chapter One

F ire Chief Will MacKenzie had just gotten off the phone with the county fire commissioner when his administrative assistant poked her head around the door of his office.

"Kara Lockwood, from the Mason Jar, called again. The reopening inspection was on your calendar this week." The fifty-something woman chewed her lip. "And it's Friday afternoon…"

He'd spent the better part of a frustrating week in back-to-back conferences with the mayor and the town council, arguing against shutting down the Truelove fire station.

But it wasn't looking good. If the proposal went forward, he'd have to uproot his son again. Health-wise, Maddox had come so far. Relocating could set back his three-year-old son, socially and emotionally. He scrubbed his forehead.

And yes, the fire safety inspection had slipped his mind. Newly remodeled and under new ownership, the restaurant couldn't reopen Saturday without his inspection.

The Mason Jar was an iconic Truelove landmark. A place to eat and also to enjoy community. The diner's months-long closure had been a sore trial to the town. Its new owner a source of great speculation. And the reopening, highly anticipated.

"My fault." Grabbing a clipboard, he pushed back his chair. "Should anyone need to reach me, you know where I'll be."

Nadine followed him into the outer office. "Then you'll head home, right?"

He glanced at his office. "I really should—"

"You're not going to solve this budget crisis today, Chief." She wagged her finger. "Your father will be home from radiation. Enjoy your weekend with Maddox and recharge your batteries."

Working with the department since his dad was chief, Nadine Phillips sometimes forgot he wasn't still Rick MacKenzie's teenage son.

At thirty-one, Will was Truelove's youngest fire chief. But he came from a long line of firefighters. A year ago when the fire chief, who had replaced his dad, opted to take a job with a larger department in North Carolina, he'd jumped at the chance to come home with his son and ailing father to Truelove.

But home was proving more elusive to find than he'd anticipated.

"Hang in there." She sat down at her desk. "God will make a way."

Will slumped. "Even when there seems to be no way forward?"

"God works in ways we cannot see." She rested her hands in her lap. "Prepare to be amazed."

He'd settle for life returning to normal. Or as normal as it could be with his dad battling cancer and his son starting to ask why everyone else had a mommy but him.

But how did Will explain to his young son that his mother had walked away without a backward glance? Liz hadn't even waited for Maddox to be released from the NICU before she moved on without either of them.

Nadine looked at him over her monitor. "Keep the faith, Chief."

Easier said than done. It wasn't that he didn't believe in God, because he did. There were no atheists in flame-engulfed buildings.

But somehow, in the bitterness of his wife's desertion, watching first his son and then Pops suffer, he'd become disconnected from God. Lost in a smoky haze. And he wasn't sure how to find his way back to Him.

"Think I'll walk to the diner."

Nadine nodded. "Good idea. Clear your head. See you Monday morning."

Heading through the open bay, he set out across the village green for the beloved diner. Despite the leafing of the old oaks lining both sides of the square in mid-March, spring hadn't yet managed to fully throw off winter's chill.

Forming a horseshoe around the small town nestled in the foothills of the Blue Ridge Mountains, the river gushed with a heavy spring runoff. His heart felt as cold as the severe, snow-laden winter from which Truelove only recently emerged.

Clipboard under his arm, he crossed Main Street. Finding the front entrance bolted, he glanced at his watch. Perhaps he should've phoned ahead. But safety inspections were best unannounced and unscheduled.

He peered inside. A light shone through the porthole window of the kitchen door. He rapped his knuckles on the glass-fronted entrance.

Will knocked again. Louder and more insistently this time. The porthole door swung open. Backlit against the kitchen lights, a slender, silhouetted figure appeared.

The woman flipped a light switch. Standing on the other

side of the glass, he got his first look at the new manager of the Mason Jar. Kara Lockwood wasn't what he'd expected.

She wore her blond hair in a simple, straight style that skimmed her jawline and framed her heart-shaped face. Her complexion creamy, there was a hint of color on her lips. And unusual for casual, mountain living, she wore a breezy pink skirt that reminded him of spring. But her eyes were as purply-blue as ripened summer blueberries.

He pointed to the TFD badge pinned to his uniform and raised the clipboard. She hurried to unlock the door and let him inside. A bell jangled above his head.

"I'm Chief Will MacKenzie."

She motioned him farther into the front dining area. "I was afraid you weren't coming today."

Wow, she was pretty. Very petite. Rather delicate-looking. At six feet tall, he towered over her.

"I meant to do the inspection earlier in the week, but first it was one thing." It wasn't like him to be so verbal. "Then another. And…" *Just stop talking already.*

She tapped her finger on her chin. "I would imagine that whole fighting fires thing keeps you busy, too." She smiled.

A strange yearning arose inside him. Something he hadn't felt in a long time.

He shuffled his feet. "I'm sorry about the delay."

Cherry blossoms cascaded across the fabric of her skirt. And a miniature Eiffel Tower.

She tucked a tendril of hair behind her ear. "No harm. As long as the Mason Jar opens tomorrow morning."

He frowned. "I'm afraid I can't promise that. The restaurant may fail to meet the safety codes."

She bristled. "It's crucial that the Mason Jar reopen on time."

"You will have to resolve any code violation issues before I can authorize the reopening."

She lifted her chin. "Why do you assume there will be issues?"

There were always issues when dealing with an attractive woman. Outside the line of duty, he steered clear of romantic entanglements. *Been there. Done that. Never again.*

"Let's get this inspection started, shall we, Ms. Lockwood?"

Kara tried not to take his all-business demeanor personally.

And yes, the fire chief was handsome. Incredibly so with his dark, brooding looks. Short, dark hair. Dark brown eyes. Strong, square jawline. Much younger than she'd expected. Only three or four years older than she was.

His open-collared white shirt reflected nicely against the smooth tan of his corded neck. Yep. He was *extremely* handsome.

If she was into that sort of thing. Which she wasn't. With her culinary dream nearly within reach, she didn't have time for a social life.

The contractors had finished the last items on the punch list yesterday. Thankfully, the paint fumes had dissipated. There remained only the piney scent of the industrial-strength cleaner she'd used to mop the black-and-white-tiled floor.

Chief MacKenzie stopped behind the counter and cast what felt to her like a critical gaze over the refurbished dining area. But maybe she was being oversensitive. She hadn't changed much in the classic, homey decor. The last thing she wanted was to put off loyal customers. She'd saved most of her changes for the menu.

It was odd she and the fire chief hadn't crossed paths

before. But perhaps, not so odd. She was a newcomer and up to her bouillabaisse in renovations. He was obviously a busy person.

She'd sunk every dime she possessed and then some into the café. But if the Mason Jar didn't pass inspection, she didn't know what she would do. She'd run out of time and money.

Before she could stop herself, she checked his conspicuously bare ring finger. Which most likely meant nothing. Maybe jewelry went against a firefighter code.

Or perhaps some men didn't wear their wedding ring. Not that she would know. In her quest to build a professional resumé, she'd never had much time for relationships.

She ushered him into the commercial-grade kitchen.

He inspected the electrical panel. "You've labeled the circuits." He ticked off an item on his clipboard. "No exposed wiring. Good."

Over the next thirty minutes, the chief checked the sprinkler system, the fire alarm and the kitchen hood exhaust system. "Please show me where you've stored the fire extinguishers."

After he inspected the extinguishers, she brought him into the supply room. He gave the large cardboard box in the middle of the floor a disapproving glance.

She knotted her hands together. "I was putting away the contents when you arrived."

He didn't say anything, but made a jot on the clipboard. Her heart pounded.

She'd worked in restaurants her entire adult life. But this was her first time facing the clipboard as an owner. She'd never had as much at stake. Chief MacKenzie had the power to shut down her dreams before they ever got off the ground.

"I'll need to examine the exits." He bent over the clipboard. "They must be well lit, accessible and clearly identified at all times."

"There's only the front entrance and this back—"

"Yoo-hoo!" The kitchen door swung open. "Kara? Deliveries to make." Pleasantly plump ErmaJean Hicks's denim-blue eyes widened. "And Chief MacKenzie, too. How marvelous!"

A small, adorable little boy peeked from behind the old woman.

Even if the child hadn't been wearing a red plastic firefighter hat and a black T-shirt proudly declaring Firefighter in Training, Kara would've guessed straightaway the dark-eyed, dark-haired boy had to be connected to Fire Chief MacKenzie.

Will stiffened. "Maddox? Where's Pops?" He looked from his son to ErmaJean. "What's going on?"

"After your dad got home from radiation, I told him Maddox and I would be fine for a few more hours until you were off duty. Rick needed to rest." Round as an apple, ErmaJean hugged his son to her side. "We had errands to run, didn't we?"

Will's stomach knotted. The radiation had taken a toll on his once-vibrant father. "I'm sorry, Miss ErmaJean. You should've called me. You've done so much already. Watching over Maddox whenever Pops has a treatment."

Divorced, married or spinster, the *Miss* was an honorary title of respect bestowed on any Southern lady who was your elder.

"Not a problem. Maddox and I had a lovely afternoon." She smiled at his son. "Snickerdoodle cookies were involved. He's a good helper in the kitchen."

He reached for Maddox. "Thank you, Miss ErmaJean, but I'll take it from here."

"Nonsense. Maddox and I wouldn't dream of interrupting, Chief." The seventy-something woman gave Kara an oh-so-innocent glance. "Especially when you're working."

He stifled a groan. Just what he didn't need. For the old woman to get the wrong idea about him and the Mason Jar manager.

ErmaJean was a member of the Double Name Club. But at least today she wasn't accompanied by her other two accomplices in matchmaking mayhem—GeorgeAnne Allen and IdaLee Moore.

The elderly ladies were infamous for poking their noses where they didn't belong. They took the town motto—Truelove, Where True Love Awaits—a little too seriously.

He brandished the clipboard like a shield. "Ms. Lockwood and I just finished with the fire safety inspection."

"Ms. Lockwood? Why so formal?" ErmaJean's brow rose. "Don't tell me this is the first time you two have met?"

Will didn't like the speculative gleam in her eyes. "We— I—"

"How remiss I've been in not introducing you before now. But with the chief such a frequent Mason Jar customer, I expect you'll be seeing lots of each other."

Before the diner closed for renovations, he'd been a regular for breakfast and lunch.

ErmaJean winked at them. "I can't wait to tell GeorgeAnne and IdaLee." She rubbed her blue-veined hands together. "They'll be tickled purple."

Kara cocked her head. "Tell them what?"

Someone ought to warn newcomers about the Truelove matchmakers. Create a public service announcement. For the safety and well-being of all concerned.

The three older women were a force of nature not to be deterred. They were determined to help everyone find their true love—whether the couple wanted a happily-ever-after or not.

In his case, definitely not.

Yet, braver hearts than his had tried and failed to avoid the Double Name Club's matchmaking machinations.

Maddox tugged at Kara's skirt. "Hi," he whispered.

She crouched beside him. "Hello there."

Maddox stuck his thumbs in the belt loops of his jeans. "What's your name?"

"Kara." She smiled. "What's yours?"

"Maddox." Lifting his hand, he touched a strand of her hair. "You're very prwetty, Miss Karwa."

Her cheeks pinked. "Thank you, Maddox."

"Do you havc a wittle boy at home?"

"No, I don't." The corner of her mouth upturned. "But if I did, I'd want him to be just like you."

Okay, score one for the new manager. She liked children. And judging from his usually slow-to-warm son, she was good with kids.

"Dis kitchen is de biggest kitchen I ever saw." Maddox gave the commercial kitchen an appraising glance. "Are you a good cooker, Miss Karwa?"

Will smiled.

She glanced over the little boy's head to ErmaJean. "As a matter of fact, there are quite a few people who've been known to travel miles to sample my food, sweetie pie."

Kara had a very attractivc mouth. Feeling a tad sucker punched, his smile fell. What was it with him today?

Wait. *Her* food?

He narrowed his eyes. Manager or chef? The Jar had always been a small-town operation. Perhaps she was both.

Maddox perked. "I have de greatest idea ever."

It was good to see his son so happy. "What's your great idea?"

He could live to be a hundred and never forget the heart-breaking sight of his preemie son hooked up to tubes and beeping monitors. Nor would he forget how alone he'd felt as the sole parent forced to make life and death decisions on his behalf.

"Miss Karwa could be our cooker." Maddox grabbed Will's sleeve. "She can be your wife. Then you won't be sad anymore, and I won't go hungwy." His son turned to Kara. "Can I be your wittle boy?"

"Maddox," he sputtered.

"Out of the mouths of babes," ErmaJean tittered.

"You do not go hungry, Maddox." He felt the heat creeping up his neck underneath his collar. "And I'm not sad."

"Pops and Daddy are bad cookers." Maddox touched Kara's arm. "Can you live at my house, Miss Karwa?"

Will took hold of Maddox's shoulder. "I do not need a wife, son. And anyway, that's not how it works."

Maddox's eyebrows bunched together like a pair of twin caterpillars. "How does it work, den?"

"Do explain it to us, Chief." ErmaJean gave Will's cheek a pat. "Nothing to be ashamed of. From time to time, we can all use help. That's what friends are for."

Time to beat a hasty retreat. Before Miss ErmaJean had him and Kara Lockwood matrimonially hog-tied.

He was surprised the old women hadn't already tried to bushwhack him. Maybe Pops, who was related to half the town, had put the warning out about him. The old saying, a burned child dreads the fire, had never felt so accurate.

ErmaJean withdrew a Mason jar from the voluminous quilted tote hanging on her shoulder. "Here's the chow-chow I promised you for opening day."

Rising, Kara moved to take the jar from her. "Thank you, Miss ErmaJean."

The older woman smiled. "In the Blue Ridge, we add

it to everything from pulled pork sandwiches to hot dogs to deviled eggs."

"*Chou* from the French for *cabbage*. Also perfect for omelets, sausages or as a relish for a charcuterie board." Kara held the red-flecked green contents of the jar to the light. "I can't wait to experiment."

In his experience, change rarely brought anything good.

"Charcuterie?" He scowled. "Whatever happened to plain ole good food? Don't tell me you've tampered with the menu, too."

She sniffed. "Good food doesn't have to be plain ole anything. I'm going for a fresh, new approach."

He grimaced. "If it ain't broke, don't fix it."

The pretty chef-manager drew herself up—all five foot two of her. "I sincerely hope your opinions regarding the cuisine didn't influence the results of the inspection."

"Of course it didn't." He squared his jaw. "I'm a professional."

She jutted her chin. "So am I."

He removed the triplicate form from the clipboard, ripped off her copy and handed it to her. "The diner passed with flying colors."

"You mean the café." Pursing her lips, she laid the paper on the stainless steel prep counter with a flourish. "Magnificent."

He folded his arms across his chest. "I can't tell you how glad I am that you're pleased."

They glared at each other.

"Well, well, well." ErmaJean gave a low, throaty chuckle. "Looks like my work here is done. You kids have fun." Waggling her fingers, she sidled through the door, which swung shut behind her.

For a few seconds a brittle tension crackled between them.

Maddox inched closer. "I wike de green chow jam, Miss Karwa."

Her face softened.

"A gentleman with exquisite taste." She threw Will a teasing grin. "The Truelove Fire Department is recruiting awfully young these days, Chief."

He gave her a wry look. "I guess since my son has taken the liberty of asking you to marry me, you should probably call me Will."

She tilted her head. "And since it appears I'll be saving your son from starvation, perhaps you should call me Kara."

Two dimples appeared in her cheeks. A sensation, not unlike freefalling, hit him square between the eyes.

A loud clatter sounded in the alley behind the restaurant.

Startled, Maddox threw his arms around Kara.

As Maddox snuggled against her, something inside Kara warmed.

Bending down, she hugged him back. His hair smelled of baby shampoo and... She searched her culinary memory for the right ingredient.

Snickerdoodles. She bit back a smile. Maddox Mac-Kenzie smelled like snickerdoodles.

"What's dat noise?" he whispered in her ear.

She sighed. "It's that cat again."

He removed his arms from around her neck. "I want to see your cat, Miss Karwa."

"It's not my cat. It's just a stray that keeps showing up."

Will placed his hand on Maddox's head. "We should go."

"Not till we see de cat, Daddy." He tugged at his father's hand. "Pwease?"

She shook her head at Will. "Who could resist such melted chocolate eyes?"

He made a face. "When it's late and he doesn't want to go to bed, it becomes easier than you'd think."

Maddox bobbed on the toes of his shoes. "Just one minute?"

"All right, but only a minute. I'm sure Kara has a million things to do before her big day tomorrow." He smiled. Small lines crinkled from the corners of his eyes.

Maddox wasn't the only one with irresistible melted chocolate eyes.

Her throat inexplicably tightening, she pushed the metal bar to open the exit door. Will held it for her and Maddox to step into the alley.

Another thud sounded. A stray feline poked its head around the green plastic trash bin. The cat made a move as if to dash inside the building, but she quickly pulled the door shut behind her. "Oh, no, you don't."

Maddox clasped his hands under his chin. "Wook at de kitty cat."

"Use your inside voice, son. We don't want to scare… him."

Kara folded her arms. "It's a him?"

Will squinted at the cat. "It's a him."

"He's bee-you-ti-ful," Maddox whispered.

"I guess what they say is true." Will grunted. "Beauty is definitely in the eye of the beholder."

She had to agree.

Dirty and not much to look at, the cream-colored tabby sat on its haunches. The feline appeared for the first time a week ago. And though she shooed it away when she closed up each night, the stray kept coming back.

"The tabby looks young." At her questioning glance, Will shrugged. "My late mother had a succession of cats."

Maddox squatted in front of the tabby.

"Whoa." Will shifted. "The cat may not like you getting so close."

Yet, the cat didn't appear unduly alarmed by their proximity.

"Behind the New Orleans restaurant where I interned, the stray cats fled at the first sign of humans." Tucking her skirt around her, Kara knelt beside Maddox. "I'd guess this cat hasn't been feral very long. Although I never had a pet of my own, so I don't know much about felines."

"I've never had a pet of my own, either." Maddox flicked his melted chocolate eyes at his father. "I wish I had a pet."

"When you're older." Will leaned against the rough brick wall. "So far, taking care of you has been all I can manage."

"I lived in de hospital dis many months." Maddox held up six fingers. "I have a big scar on my chest."

She locked eyes with Will.

"Maddox was in a hurry to meet the world. He was born early. It was touch and go for a while."

"I'm so sorry," she murmured. "How frightening that must've been."

"Yeah," he rasped. "It was."

Dragging his gaze away, he focused on some far distant point. "All's well that ends well."

There'd been no mention of Maddox's mother. Had she died giving birth to him? How awful, leaving Will to cope with Maddox's preemie issues as a single, grief-stricken parent.

Her heart went out to him. "And now your father is sick with cancer, too?"

"The hits just keep coming." He gave her a grim smile. "Life hasn't been easy."

"Not for me, either."

She could see the questions forming in his eyes. But her childhood was a subject best avoided.

Propping her hands on her thighs, she rose. "If I'd had a pet, though, it wouldn't have been a cat."

The tabby meowed.

"De kitty cat's hungwy." Maddox rubbed his face against her skirt. "Me, too."

Will pushed off the wall. "Maddox."

Kara smiled. "I think I could find something around the café for a starving young man like yourself."

She understood more than most about food insecurity. It was not in her DNA to let any creature go hungry.

Kara jabbed her finger at the cat. "If I give you food, you'll stay out of my trash cans, right?"

The tabby stared up at her with its unnerving green eyes.

"As long as we have a deal…" She punched in the security code. "But you can't come inside, kitty cat. There are rules about that sort of thing, right, Chief MacKenzie?"

Lips twitching, he planted his hands on his hips. "There are indeed."

"Stay here, kitty cat," she called over her shoulder. "I'll fix you a dish." Maddox and Will followed her into the kitchen.

The fire chief probably thought she was an idiot for talking to a cat.

She retrieved a white chef's apron from the peg inside her office. "I was testing the oven this morning and baked a batch of chocolate éclairs that will go to waste if someone doesn't eat them."

Kara tied the apron around her waist. "Do you know anyone who might volunteer to taste test them for me?"

Maddox raised his hand. "Me! Pick me! I'll taste dem for you."

She and Will exchanged amused glances. "That is so kind of you, sweetie. As long as your father says it's okay. I'd hate for it to spoil your father's plans for dinner."

The child blinked. "What plan?"

Will shrugged his broad shoulders. She did her best to drag her eyes from the muscles rippling underneath his shirt.

Be still her heart... Who could resist a firefighter?

Will gave her a sheepish grin. "At this moment the boy is not wrong about there being no plan for dinner."

She dragged over a footstool so Maddox could wash his hands under the faucet at the giant prep sink. "Can I fix you something to eat, Will?"

"I'll wait for when you're up and running. Get the full effect."

Maddox quickly consumed the éclair. "Dat was yummy." He licked his lips. "Dis is why we need her, Daddy."

She laughed. Will rolled his eyes. She pulled out a few eggs from the refrigerator.

Chocolate encircling his mouth, Maddox dogged her steps. "Can I cook wid you?"

"Of course you can, young chef." Under her watchful eye, he helped her break the eggs and beat the yolks.

Will leaned against the counter. "Why eggs?"

"Good source of protein." It didn't take long to scramble the eggs in the skillet. "Tell me you'll give this sweetie pie some protein for dinner."

He raised his palm. "On my firefighter's honor, I solemnly pledge to give Sweetie Pie, also known as Maddox William MacKenzie, protein for dinner."

The little boy doubled over with laughter. "Y'all awe so siwee."

She and Will smiled at each other.

Kara transferred the steaming eggs to a white porcelain plate. "I think somebody has the gilly-siggles."

"Probably because *somebody* gave him too much sugar." Will smirked.

"Can we feed de kitty cat now?"

"Sure." She filled a saucer with water. "But the cat is probably long gone." Handing the eggs to Maddox, she took charge of the saucer.

Will pushed open the exit door.

To her surprise, she found the cat exactly where they'd left him. Waiting for them. No, that was crazy. The cat was waiting for food.

Maddox set the plate on the pavement. She placed the saucer beside the eggs. The stray tensed. But when she stepped back, the cat sprang forward.

Standing shoulder to shoulder, she and Will watched Maddox watch the cat. The little boy was so, so sweet.

"I think he's holding his breath," Will whispered.

His breath fluttered a wisp of hair dangling at her ear. And set off brisk palpitations in her heart.

The tabby devoured the eggs. Its little pink tongue lapped up the water. The cat meowed.

"You're welcome." She reached for the plate. "My first satisfied customer."

But with a flick of its tail, the stray raced away.

Maddox waved. "Bye-bye, kitty cat."

The tabby disappeared around the corner of the building.

Air leached from her lungs in a slow trickle between her lips. "Now, if only the fine citizens of Truelove will love my cooking tomorrow." There was a lot riding on the success of this venture.

Will riffled his son's hair. "Tell Miss Kara thank you for the éclair."

"Dank you, Miss Karwa." Maddox threw himself at her.

"Easy, son." Will winced at the chocolate stain on her apron. "The not-so-pristine life of a preschooler. Sorry about that. But better the apron than the skirt."

She kissed the top of his son's head. "Doesn't matter. Occupational hazard. For a Maddox hug, I'd call it a fair exchange."

An emotion flitted across his face, but was gone too quickly for her to decipher.

"We better go check on Pops, Maddox." His tone brusque, he studied his shoes. And she decided she must have imagined the expression in his eyes.

She punched in the code and jerked open the back door. "Would it be okay if I sent the remaining éclairs to your father?"

"Pops would love that." He took Maddox's hand. "Thank you."

Kara boxed the pastries and handed them to Maddox to give to his grandfather. Will retrieved his clipboard.

She escorted them into the front dining room. "Have a good evening."

"You, too." He'd seemed in a hurry to leave, but now he lingered at the entrance. "And Kara?"

She took a quick breath. "Yes?"

He stared at her for a second, then rubbed the back of his neck. "Despite the sleepy, small-town charm, bolt the door after us."

She had the impression he'd been about to say something else, but changed his mind.

The bell jangled as he yanked open the front door. "In a town the size of Truelove, I guess we're bound to run into each other again sooner or later." He steered his son outside, and the door closed behind them.

She sagged against the register. *Hallelujah and thank*

you, Chief MacKenzie. The Mason Jar would reopen on schedule.

Above the ridge of encircling mountains, bold streaks of apricot, plum and raspberry burnished the dusky twilight of the sky.

Yet, as she watched father and son pick their way across the town square toward the fire station, it wasn't tomorrow's opening that worried her.

It was the way her heart leaped at the idea of seeing the fire chief sooner rather than later that troubled her the most.

Chapter Two

The next morning it was still dark when Kara arrived at the café.

She shivered, but not only from the cold. Feeling more than a little scared and alone, she inserted the key in the lock and unbolted the door. Stepping inside, she flicked on the overhead light.

The bell jangled again. Her heart jerking, she swung around.

Sixty-five years old and African American, Glorieta Ferguson wagged her finger. "I don't care if you think Truelove, North Carolina, is the next best thing to Mayberry, missy. If you're going to be here alone, that door needs to be locked."

"What're you doing here? And at four a.m.?" Kara rushed forward to embrace her foster mother. "Did you drive from Durham this morning?"

"I drove in last night. And since you've only one bedroom in the house you rented, I got a motel room on the highway." Glorieta pursed her lips. "You didn't think I'd let my business partner and best girl suffer through opening-day jitters alone, did you?"

Kara gave her a cockeyed look. "I don't believe you've ever suffered a single opening-day jitter in your life."

Glorieta raised her brow. "Not true."

"At the opening of restaurant number five?" Kara rolled her eyes to the ceiling. "Or was it restaurant number six?"

Miss Glorieta's Down Home Barbecue and Fixins—or Miss G's, as the restaurant chain was affectionately called by everyone from the governor to sanitation truck employees—was a North Carolina institution. One president had called her a national treasure. And her secret recipe barbecue sauce, sold at fine grocery establishments, was legendary.

Her mentor unbuttoned her coat. "Each and every one was like birthing another child."

Over the past two years, the barbecue queen had stepped back from the business, and had attempted to learn golf, grow orchids and paint landscapes. All to no avail. In their last phone conversation, Glorieta had indicated she was taking up bridge. Must not be going well.

"We agreed you would be a silent investor, Mama G."

"You and the boys agreed." Defiance gleamed from her dark eyes. "I agreed to nothing."

The *boys* were her two grown sons, who'd taken over running their mother's food empire. They'd been overjoyed at the prospect of Kara's business proposition. Anything to get their well-meaning, never-stop-meddling mother out of their corporate hair.

"You're supposed to be enjoying the good life." Kara shook her head. "You don't have to work so hard anymore."

"Worst decision I ever made was retiring. I'm sick to death of this lady of leisure stuff." Her double chin quivered. "Unless you don't want me here."

She'd never meant to make the older woman feel unwanted.

Once upon a terrible time, Kara had been a half-starved little girl. Lured by tantalizing smells of roasted meat, she'd crept into then-middle-aged Glorieta's kitchen. And instead of turning her out, the woman in the African geometric-print chef's hat had welcomed her. Eventually teaching Kara everything she knew about food and life.

But more important, Glorieta had loved her. After Kara's ailing mother died and no one else wanted her, Glorieta had opened not only her heart to Kara, but her home, as well.

She owed Glorieta everything. Which only increased the pressure she felt—emotionally and fiscally—to make the Mason Jar a success.

Kara leaned into her strength. "Actually, it wouldn't be a bad idea to have someone oversee the orders while I supervise the dining room. Or vice versa."

Glorieta smiled. "I'd be honored to make sure the kitchen runs smoothly."

A weight lifted off Kara's shoulders. "Thank you for coming."

"When does the rest of your crew arrive?"

"Leo, my short-order cook, should be here momentarily. The waitresses, Shayla and Trudy, come at five. We'll open the door at six."

The full-figured woman squared her shoulders. "Sounds like a plan."

Glorieta had started with nothing. But through hard work, perseverance and faith, the single mother of two had let nothing stand in her way to becoming a successful restaurateur. And it was from Glorieta she learned the deeply satisfying joy of feeding people.

Her throat clogged with emotion. "I love you."

Glorieta kissed her forehead. "Love you, too."

Her eyes watered.

"But no more of that." Glorieta became brisk. "Put me to work."

At 6:00 a.m., customers lined the block outside. Kara's stomach did a flip. For the next few hours she didn't have time to do anything but greet, seat and assist her waitstaff with the orders.

She'd scheduled the soft opening over the weekend, to work out the kinks before facing the heavier weekday traffic.

When the former owner had decided to sell the diner, Kara had offered to keep his staff. Only fifty-something, brassy-blonde Trudy had stayed. Which Kara wasn't sure was a blessing or a curse. But the wiry-thin woman, overly fond of tanning beds, was as much an institution as the Mason Jar itself.

The upside was Trudy knew everyone in town. And Kara was counting on Trudy to help her get to know the locals. The downside was Trudy wasn't shy about voicing her objections to changes.

Kara only hoped the rest of Truelove wasn't as set in their ways.

Midmorning, Trudy introduced her to the pastor at the community church.

Reverend Bryant had a kind, scholarly face. "I hope you'll join us Sunday morning."

Once when she was a child, her family had traveled to the church for Homecoming Sunday. Sometimes she felt like she'd been searching for home ever since.

She remembered Truelove as a friendly, hospitable community. The kind of place where neighbors cared for one another. The best sort of place to not only operate a business, but also to put down deep roots and call home. And that was what Truelove felt like to her—like coming home.

Kara handed the pastor a menu. "I'd love that."

Thus far, her weekends hadn't lent themselves to taking Sunday off. But starting tomorrow with the opening behind her, she meant to rectify that.

Some customers had questions regarding menu changes. But smoothing over the missing items, she drew their attention to similar entrées. After diving into their food, everyone seemed pleased with her recommendations.

A steady stream of patrons arrived for brunch. Wisecracking Trudy was in her element. Filling water glasses and topping off coffee mugs, she maintained a lighthearted banter with the diners. Kara kept a careful eye on her other waitress, Shayla.

Something about the girl brought out her maternal instincts. Which was ridiculous, considering Kara was probably only five years older. Yet, despite keeping chatter to a minimum, Shayla proved to be a hard worker. Not everyone needed to be as talkative as Trudy.

Behind the counter in her chef whites, Glorieta reached for a porcelain mug on the warming rack. "Thought I'd grab a coffee and take a quick break."

She touched Glorieta's sleeve. "You're not overdoing it, are you?"

"Absolutely not. I just wanted to enjoy your success. You should do the same."

"When the last diner leaves, I will." Kara took a quick survey of the dining area. "Right now I'm going to check on my customers."

Glorieta patted her shoulder. "Good girl. Work the room."

Moving away, Kara fluttered her fingers. "Something else I learned from you."

Around one o'clock, ErmaJean bustled through the door with her two Double Name companions in tow. Menus in hand, Kara met them at the register.

ErmaJean's denim-blue eyes sparkled. "Happy opening day, dear cousin!"

She and ErmaJean weren't cousins. At least, not by blood. Her father had grown up in Truelove and had been distantly related to ErmaJean's deceased husband. However, in the Southern way of family reckoning, that qualified as close kin.

A few weeks ago their paths had crossed at the post office. Remembering Kara from that Homecoming Sunday years ago, the older woman had embraced Kara like a long-lost relative. She'd taken Kara under her wing and introduced her to the Double Name Club.

"Welcome to the Mason Jar Café, ladies."

As tall and spare as ErmaJean was round, GeorgeAnne Allen pushed her black horn-rimmed glasses higher on the bridge of her long, bony nose. "Don't see any use in changing a perfectly good name like *diner* for *café*."

Kara's smile dimmed a shade. GeorgeAnne's family owned the local hardware store. The faintly terrifying woman—with her ice-blue eyes and short, iron-gray cap of hair—was the uncontested leader of the matchmaker pack.

But retired schoolteacher IdaLee Moore, the oldest and most diminutive of the ladies, shushed her fellow matchmaker. "Don't be contrary, GeorgeAnne."

Kara readjusted her smile. "Why don't we get you ladies settled?"

Drawing them into the dining room, she ignored Trudy, who was frantically waving her hands. Kara stopped beside an empty booth. "Here we are."

GeorgeAnne stiffened. "That's *not* where we usually sit."

"But this booth has such a lovely view of the square."

GeorgeAnne folded her arms across her green denim jacket. "It's *not* our table."

ErmaJean and IdaLee exchanged anxious looks.

The matchmakers had a table? She wished someone had told her. She glanced over to Trudy. Okay, maybe Trudy had tried.

Clutching napkin-wrapped utensils, Trudy scurried from behind the counter and stationed herself beside a table on the far wall underneath the community bulletin board. She arched her heavily plucked eyebrows at Kara.

Thank you, Trudy. She'd just earned her keep and then some.

Kara motioned. "Seems we have your regular table ready now."

GeorgeAnne harrumphed. "I should think so." And plowed her way across the crowded diner.

ErmaJean gave Kara a thumbs-up. Leaving them in Trudy's capable hands, Kara returned to the register. Crisis averted. Barely.

A seal of approval from Truelove's Double Name Club could mean the difference between success and struggling to stay afloat.

She glanced out the window and spotted Maddox on the sidewalk with an older man she guessed must be Pops.

Both gazed across the square at the fire station. Perhaps they were waiting for Will to join them.

Suddenly more nervous than when she opened this morning, she headed for the safety zone of the kitchen.

Will had gotten the call before the sun topped the ridge.

Back at the station hours later and feeling more than a physical weariness, he changed out of his turnout gear into a clean pair of bunker pants and a long-sleeved TFD T-shirt. After taking out his phone, he shot off a text to alert his father he was finally on his way to meet them for a late lunch.

Crossing the street, he spotted Maddox and Pops waiting for him outside the restaurant. Rushing forward, his son hugged him around the knees.

The fire fatalities flashed through his mind.

Swallowing hard, he hugged Maddox tighter than usual. His son made a quick grab for his firefighter hat to keep it from sliding off his head.

Pops gave Will a concerned look. "Rough call?"

"A family with two kids. We were too late."

Pops winced. "It's not an easy job. But try to remember what you do matters."

Maddox grabbed his hand. "Come on, Daddy. We're on a mission."

"What kind of mission?"

"A wunch mission. My tummy's hungwy for mac and cheese. Are you up for dis mission, Chief MacKenzie?"

"I'm up for it, Probationary Firefighter Maddox."

The bell jangled above the door as they stepped into the Mason Jar. The pleasing aroma of freshly baked bread floated past his nostrils.

"Some-ding smells yummy." Maddox bounced in his sneakers. "Yummy to my tummy."

Heads turned at his son's not-so-inside voice.

The diner was jam-packed. In jeans and pink Mason Jar T-shirts, Trudy and a young woman he recognized from the trailer park on the other side of the river hurried from table to table with heavily loaded trays.

He realized he was scoping out the restaurant for Kara.

"Wook, Daddy!" Maddox pressed both hands against the glass pastry case. "I want dat one, Pops." His big, dark eyes widened. "And dat one, too."

Pops chuckled.

Kara came out of the kitchen. "Oh, hi."

Was it his imagination or had she blushed?

She extended her hand to his dad. "I'm Kara Lockwood. You three wouldn't by any chance be related to each other, would you?"

Grinning, Pops shook her hand. "Guilty as charged. I'm Rick MacKenzie, Will's father. Smoke eating runs in our veins."

She gathered the menus. "Three for lunch?"

Will nodded and removed the firefighter hat from his son's head.

Maddox held up three fingers. "I'm fwee."

She hugged him. "And the most wonderful three-year-old I've ever met."

Maddox beamed.

Weaving her way among the tables scattered across the room, she led them to an empty booth across from the matchmakers.

His dad slid into one side of the booth. On the other side, Will eased in after Maddox. She laid the menus in front of them.

"One for Pops. One for me." Maddox ticked off the numbers on his pudgy little fingers. "And one for Daddy." He held up his hand again. "Fwee like me."

"You are so smart. Would you like a booster seat so you can reach your food better?"

He shook his head. "I'm big. 'Cause I'm guess what?"

Tapping her finger against her chin, she pretended to think. "You're big because you are… Twenty-five?"

He giggled into his hands. "No…"

"Oh, I'm sorry. You said you were forty-five."

Maddox erupted into laughter. "I'm fwee, Miss Karwa. Fwee."

She gave her forehead a playful smack. "Silly me."

He'd never seen his son take to a stranger so quickly.

Maddox started building a house with the sugar packets. "I want to be a cooker wike Miss Karwa when I grow up."

She removed an order pad from the pocket of her white apron. "I thought you wanted to be a firefighter."

"I want to be both." He got on his knees. "When can we cook some more, Miss Karwa?"

Will scrubbed his face with his hand. "Miss Kara is busy with the Mason Jar. She doesn't have—"

"I'd love to cook with Maddox again. Maybe one afternoon after the café closes for the day."

A knot tightened in the pit of his stomach.

He was well aware of the lack of female influence in his son's life. But more Maddox time with Kara meant more time for him with her, too. He couldn't go there. Not ever again.

To take his mind off how attractive she looked in the pale blue blouse paired with jeans, he picked up the menu. "We'll see," he grunted.

Kara's smile slipped. "Perhaps, Chief MacKenzie, you'd prefer to begin with our house specialty, café au lait?"

He'd prefer she call him Will. And he'd rather not examine his reasons too closely. "Café o'what?"

"It means coffee with milk."

He leaned forward. "I know what it means, but what happened to plain ole American coffee?"

"You can make plain ole American coffee at home."

He ran his hand over his head. "The fire department was called out to an incident, so I didn't get to have coffee at home."

She made a palms-up gesture. "Consider café au lait at the Mason Jar a call to adventure."

He hunched his shoulders. "I've had about all the excitement I can take for one day."

"But regular coffee is so...so..." She flung out her hand.

He cocked his head. "So what?"

She fluttered her lashes. "So boring."

He bit back a laugh. "Boring?"

Kara propped her hand on her hip. "I call 'em like I see 'em."

"Sounds like it's time to answer the call, son." His father winked at Kara. "I wouldn't mind trying one of those fancy coffee drinks myself."

Traitor.

She favored his father with a sweet smile.

Will stroked his jaw. "Are you telling me the Mason Jar no longer offers regular coffee?"

Her eyes sparked. *This was fun.* He gave her a crooked grin.

Pops laid aside the menu. "I'll have whatever coffee you're brewing. It smells fantastic."

"Café au lait, it is." Smirking, she scrawled a note across the order pad. "And I'll get a boring, regular American coffee for Chief MacKenzie."

He started to laugh until he noticed that several feet away, the Double Name Club appeared to be taking more than a passing interest in their conversation.

She made a jot on the order pad. "And for Master Maddox?"

"You're so funny, Miss Karwa. I want milk."

"Coming right up."

Holding his hat to his chest, Maddox wriggled down from the seat and scooted underneath the booth.

Will made a grab for his son, but he wasn't quick enough.

"I go see de kitty cat."

She placed her hand on his son's cheek. "It's busy in the kitchen, sweetheart. I don't want you to get hurt. Maybe another time, okay?"

"You pwomise?"

"I promise."

Maddox clambered into the booth, and Will slid across the seat to make room. Within minutes she returned with their drinks.

"Have you made a decision about lunch?"

Maddox propped his elbows on the table. "I want mac and cheese."

Will flipped the menu pages. "I don't see mac and cheese on here anymore," he huffed.

"But why can't I have mac and cheese?" Maddox tuned up. "You said I could have mac and cheese, Daddy." The daddy part emerged as a whine.

Will reddened. "I apologize. He's not usually so—"

"A late lunch and too little sleep can make the best of us hangry." Pops waggled his eyebrows. "And I'm not only talking about the kid."

She put a soothing hand on Maddox's back. "Mac and cheese is still on the menu. But with a different spin."

Will furrowed his brow. "Where? I don't see it."

Leaning over his son, she placed her finger on an item halfway down the page. "There."

The scent of vanilla wafted off her clothing, and his pulse sped up. "Croque-Monsieur?"

"Dat's not mac and cheese."

"It's better." She squeezed Maddox's hand. "Southern comfort food with a French twist." She looked at Will. "The Mason Jar has a new policy that if customers don't like their food, the meal is on the house."

He settled against the cushion. "The owner must have a lot of confidence to make an offer like that."

She gave him an odd look. "The *owner* has a lot of confidence in her food. Croque-Monsieur Mac and Cheese is one of my favorites." She touched Maddox's arm. "Will you try it, sweetie pie?"

Rubbing his eyes, Maddox gave a slow nod. "I trwy for you."

She smiled. "You're going to love it. And what about your dad and granddad?"

Pops pointed to the daily special chalked onto the blackboard over the cut-out window behind the counter. "What's this croquet madame thingy?"

"The Croque-Madame is a ham sandwich covered in cheese and an egg."

"Simpler if the menu just said that," Will muttered.

Pen poised over the pad, she bared her teeth at him. "And what about you, Chief MacKenzie?"

She was very cute when she got riled. It was kind of fun pushing her buttons.

His lips quirked. "I'm not sure what *Chief MacKenzie* wants. Why don't you ask *Will* what he would like?"

"All right." She cut her eyes at him. "What would *Will* like?"

To know you better. He hadn't said that out loud, had he?

He flushed. "Uh… What would you recommend?"

"You look like a meat and potatoes guy."

Pops hooted. "Pegged you in one."

He glared at his father. Pops laughed.

Kara pointed to the board. "How about the beef bourguignon?"

"Sounds great." He closed the menu. "Of course, you had me at *beef.*"

The indigo in her eyes deepened. "Good to know." And she gave him a sweet smile all his own.

For a second, reality went sideways. *Wow.* Seriously, those dimples ought to be registered as lethal weapons.

After collecting their menus, she disappeared into the

kitchen, and Maddox returned to fiddling with the sugar packets.

Will scanned the refurbished restaurant. "The diner's different."

Pops took a sip of coffee. "Not too different. Just spruced up."

"It doesn't look like our Mason Jar."

Pops eyed him over the rim of the mug. "Only if you prefer foam stuffing coming out of cracked vinyl seats. It's a new and improved version."

Bell jangling, a handful of off-duty firefighters headed inside. Will responded to their greetings. The guys grabbed stools at the counter.

Kara breezed through with their entrées. "I'll check with you later about dessert."

Pops said a quick grace, and they tucked into their lunch.

If the mouthwatering aromas were any indication, the new recipes were going to be a hit. The meat was tender. The juices flavorful. Will enjoyed every bite.

Meanwhile, Kara had become involved in appeasing the prickly GeorgeAnne over an issue with her order.

An African American lady about his father's age in a chef's coat came through the swinging door. Was she the new owner?

GeorgeAnne continued to make a fuss about her order. And like Maddox earlier, not bothering to use her inside voice. Or caring who else heard.

The lunch crowd had dwindled, but heads turned like onlookers at a car crash to watch the ensuing altercation. Behind the counter, the new owner frowned.

With a screeching scrape across the linoleum, GeorgeAnne pushed back her chair and marched toward the exit. Kara's blueberry eyes watered.

Something protective, and altogether surprising, surged inside his chest.

The owner had disappeared into the kitchen again. Was she going to let Kara put up with that kind of abuse?

He started to rise, but Pops shook his head. "Don't make it worse. You'll only embarrass her further."

IdaLee reached for the bill.

But Kara snatched it up. "I'm so sorry she didn't like it. Lunch is on me."

"I can't allow that." Her snow-white bun gleaming in the fluorescent lighting, IdaLee shook her head. "GeorgeAnne is in one of her difficult moods today."

From what he remembered of growing up in Truelove, GeorgeAnne had been in a *difficult* mood since about 1990.

"I'm so sorry this happened, Kara Lynn." ErmaJean bit her lip. "And on opening day."

"That GeorgeAnne," Pops growled.

Would the owner take the bill out of Kara's salary? *Extra big tip,* Will mouthed across the table to his father.

IdaLee held out her gnarled, blue-veined hand. As generations of Truelove schoolchildren had learned the hard way, when Miss IdaLee got that look in her eye, resistance was futile.

Although a newcomer, Kara was a quick study. She handed the bill over to the old woman.

"That was a delicious meal. I thoroughly enjoyed it." IdaLee took out her beaded wallet. "I'm not making excuses, but GeorgeAnne's rude behavior had nothing to do with you. These are unsettled times in Truelove."

Since the outlet mall opened on the highway, job opportunities had expanded. But as with most progress, there'd been a downside. Several local family-owned businesses had found themselves in jeopardy. Including the hardware store.

ErmaJean and IdaLee followed Kara to the cash register.

Yet more confusion appeared to be unfolding with his crew at the counter. Will snagged their bill off the table. "Let me out, son."

Maddox scooted out.

Will strode toward his guys, who were climbing off the stools. "Everything okay?" Sometimes emotions ran high after a call like the one this morning.

Zach, one of the volunteer firefighters, shrugged his skinny shoulders. "Too many fancy words on the menu. We decided to get real food at the Burger Depot."

Luke, a part-timer, usually the most sensible one, shuffled his feet and said nothing.

Will hoped the owner got her act together or the Mason Jar *Café* wouldn't last long in Truelove. His dad and Maddox joined him.

Pops jutted his chin at the table behind them. "Took care of what we talked about."

The bell jangled as his firefighters exited. The matchmakers followed. Will stepped up to the register.

Shoulders slumped, Kara took the bill and his credit card. "How was your meal?" A length of hair came loose from the bun at the nape of her neck and fell forward, obscuring half of her face.

He didn't like not being able to see her expressive eyes. "Fabulous."

She looked up.

He felt an almost irresistible urge to smooth the tendril out of her eyes. Will stuck his hands into his pockets. "Everything that you promised and more."

"I—I'm glad."

Maddox grabbed her around the knees. "Dat's de best croaky mac and cheese I ever ate."

A quick smile lit her features. She planted a kiss on the top of his head. "That may be the nicest thing anyone's ever said to me. You made my day."

"Let's wait for Dad outside, Maddox," Pops called from the door.

Maddox wiggled his small fingers. "Bye, Miss Karwa."

She wiggled her fingers back at him. "Bye-bye, sweet boy."

Unexpectedly, Will's heart sped up a little.

His father and son exited.

"Oh, no." Her mouth rounded. "I didn't offer y'all dessert."

"Rain check." He cocked his head. "That will give me a reason to come again."

"I—I'd like that. I mean…" She touched her hand to her throat. "I'll look forward to…"

The bottom dropped out of his stomach. "I'll look forward to it, too."

She smiled. "Till then." She handed him his credit card and receipt.

Not knowing what else to say, and feeling strangely panicked for a man who made his living running into fires, he quickly walked out the door.

What just happened?

In no way, shape or form could he possibly have felt something romantic for a woman he'd barely met. He didn't do emotion. Not after Liz. Had he learned nothing from the debacle of his marriage?

He scowled. "Maddox, you want to ride home with Pops or me?"

"With Pops." Maddox used the tip of his finger to push back his firefighter hat. "We're getting ice cweam."

His father took hold of Maddox's hand. "Want to join us?"

"No, thanks. I'm going to head home and take a nap. See you guys soon."

Only he didn't count on being waylaid in the fire station parking lot by GeorgeAnne Allen.

Zach and the station crew formed a semicircle around them.

GeorgeAnne sniffed. "It's time to take action, Chief."

Zach stuck his thumbs inside his suspenders. "The people of Truelove aren't going to take this sitting down."

"What's going on?"

She thrust the Mason Jar menu at Will.

"Read it and weep, Chief." Zach groaned.

"Where did you get this?"

She peered over the frames of her glasses at him.

"Okay, I know where you got this." He frowned. "I just can't believe you stole this from the diner."

"You mean the *café*?" GeorgeAnne rolled her eyes. "I didn't steal it. I borrowed it. Of more immediate concern is that the apple pie has been removed."

His forehead creased. "No apple pie?"

The high country of Truelove was apple country. Orchards dotted the county. The diner—at least the *old* diner—was renowned for its apple desserts.

"Look for yourself." She scrunched her face. "The new owner has taken everything we love most about the Mason Jar and changed it."

Scanning the menu, he realized GeorgeAnne was right. The apple pie, beloved by generations of Truelovers, was gone. Replaced by something called Apple Galette.

"There's been far too many changes in our town, Chief. And too many outsiders telling us what to do."

Which was rich coming from GeorgeAnne Allen, who'd spent her entire life telling everyone else exactly what they ought to do.

But she wasn't wrong about the current state of affairs. With the new jobs came an influx of newcomers. Possessing strong opinions on better ways to run everything from the library to the schools to closing the fire station.

Many folks in Truelove were feeling more than a mite sensitive. And was it any wonder? Their cherished mountain way of life appeared to be under siege.

Was the apple pie the last straw?

"The question is, Chief, what are we going to do about it?"

He scratched his head. "I don't see much we *can* do about it."

"If we allow this latest outrage to go unchallenged, what's next?" She threw out her hands. "A ban on sweet tea?"

Zach nodded. "She has a point, Chief."

He crossed his arms. "What do you have in mind?"

"After I left the Jar, I rushed home and created this petition to reinstate the apple pie." She pulled a sheaf of papers from the cavernous depths of her purse. "To be signed by the concerned citizens of Truelove."

Zach raised his hand. "I'll sign it."

She handed Will the stack of papers. "And presented by Truelove's fire chief to the new owner."

He reared. "Why me?"

"Isn't apple pie your favorite dessert, Chief?"

He rubbed the back of his neck. "It is."

She gave him a thin smile. "They respect your position. People will line up in droves to stand with you and sign the petition."

"I think you overestimate my influence in this town, Miss GeorgeAnne."

"With the proposed changes, the fire department has as much, if not more, at stake than the rest of us." She lifted her bony chin. "What better way to show how important the Truelove Fire Department is to this town than for its fire chief to take the lead on this issue?"

"The safety of Truelove and the well-being of my men has to be my priority." He shook his head. "I can't neglect our mission to run around town getting signatures."

"We'll be sure the petition makes the rounds. Say yes, Chief." Zach opened his hands. "Let's do this for True-love."

He examined their earnest, eager faces. His crew had been on edge for days. Feeling helpless to save the fire station and their jobs.

Next month the town council would vote on the proposed consolidation of the fire station with a larger county department. Would the petition demonstrate the strength of community support for the TFD? Might this be the distraction the guys needed?

"All right." He raised his hand. "But only so long as it doesn't interfere with our primary purpose as a firehouse."

"Excellent." GeorgeAnne nodded. "Apple pie will be back on the menu faster than you can say, 'Welcome to Truelove.'"

"What if the owner refuses?"

GeorgeAnne snorted. "Then we'll stage a boycott until that young miss sees sense."

Hold the fire hose. Had he missed something vital here?

A sudden, sinking feeling clawed at his gut. "Who exactly is the new owner of the Mason Jar?"

GeorgeAnne blinked at him, owl-like. "Kara Lock-wood, of course."

Oh, no. His stomach tanked. What had he committed himself to?

This wasn't going to turn out well. Not well at all.

Chapter Three

At precisely 3:00 p.m., Kara flipped the Open sign to Closed.

"That's a wrap." She did an about-face toward the dining area. "Well-done, everyone."

"Wasn't that fun?" Glorieta gave her a hug. "All in all, a successful opening day."

Except for the blip involving Miss GeorgeAnne.

"The first of many successful days." Glorieta smiled. "We sold out of croissants."

Gum-smacking Trudy hip-butted the swinging door open. "That Frenchie mac and cheese was a hit, too."

Recalling Maddox's sweet little face, Kara pushed aside the incident with GeorgeAnne Allen from her mind. Not everyone would be pleased with her food. Best to concentrate on those who would.

She checked to be sure the oven and burners were turned off. Everyone set about completing the closing protocols she'd instituted. Leo scraped the grill. Trudy scrubbed and disinfected the prep station. Shayla wiped down the last of the tables.

But Kara insisted Glorieta change out of her chef whites.

"We've got this, Mama G. Go back to the motel and rest."

Glorieta's jaw tightened. "I'm fully capable of helping you close the restaurant."

"I know you are, but…" She lowered her voice so as not to be overheard. "It's important everyone learn how to do it properly themselves. We won't always have you to do it for us."

Glorieta gazed at her a long, hard minute. "All right. Point taken. When Little Bird is ready to leave the nest, Mother Bird needs to let her fly."

Rising on her toes, she kissed the woman's plump cheek. "Thank you for everything." And by everything, she meant so much more than what Glorieta had done today.

But as usual, her foster mom waved away any sign of sentimentality. "I did what anyone else would've done."

So not true. Because no one had. Only her.

"I'll go, but only if you meet me at that barbecue place later." Glorieta wagged her finger. "For a dinner neither of us has to cook."

"Sounds like a great plan to me." She cocked her head. "But you realize in the Blue Ridge, restaurants serve Western-style barbecue."

Glorieta gave a faint shudder. "Bless their hearts. We'll call it market research." She lifted her chin. "It's always a good idea to know the competition."

Not long after she left, the rest of the crew finished their tasks and said goodbye until Monday morning.

Kara was dead on her feet, yet adrenaline hummed through her body. And she knew from experience that the peculiar rush would take a while to fade.

She spent the next half hour adding up the day's receipts in her office and checking inventory in the supply closet. After mopping the floors, she leaned against the handle.

While Mama G wasn't much for emotions, Kara felt it not only right but good to take a moment to enjoy the pine aroma. Giving herself permission to mark the milestone of all she'd accomplished. A monument of grateful remembrance to how far she'd come.

"Thank You, Lord," she whispered in the quiet.

Four o'clock might just become her favorite time of day.

Putting away the bucket, she heard a faint scratching at the back door. Her mouth curving, she retrieved the dairy-free egg soufflé from the warming tray.

She eased the door open slightly so as not to startle the cat. The cream-colored tabby looked up at her and me-owed. She set the white porcelain ramekin and the water dish on the pavement. Utilizing a broken block of cement, she propped open the door.

From the threshold, she watched the tabby sniff the soufflé. Apparently finding the offering acceptable, the cat began to eat.

Last night sleep had proven elusive for Kara. Her thoughts had flitted from worst-case opening scenarios—none of which had occurred—to a particular fire chief. She folded her arms. She still owed him a dessert. A rain check, he'd said. Rain or sunshine, she liked the sound of that.

So as not to startle the stray, she slowly lowered to a crouch.

But seemingly feeling unthreatened, the tabby moved on to the water bowl. His little pink tongue lapped at the water.

"All things bright and beautiful," she murmured. "All creatures great and small."

The words were from a hymn her mother used to sing to her when she was a child.

In an effort to distract herself last night, she'd searched online for information on cats. She'd learned most were lactose intolerant. Hence, the dairy-free version of the soufflé she'd concocted. She tilted her head. Come to think of it, the tabby was about the same color as a soufflé.

Finishing its meal, with its tail held straight in the air, the cat walked over to her. The stray surprised her by rubbing its head against her legs. Before she could react, however, the tabby dashed away down the alley out of sight.

"All things wise and wonderful," she sang as she stood upright. "The Lord God made them all."

Dinner proved entertaining with Mama G preaching the gospel of vinegar-based barbecue to all and sundry. She and the cook ended up trading tips on the best ways to baste. Glorieta also gifted the very nice gentleman with a bottle of Miss G's own barbecue sauce.

"I've done what I can," Glorieta pronounced as a laughing Kara drew her out of the restaurant. "The rest is up to their conscience and God."

The next morning she drove Glorieta to church. It was nice not having to go alone the first time. Nestled in a glade on the edge of town, the steeple brushed a picture-perfect Blue Ridge sky.

She turned into the parking lot. Gravel crunched beneath the tires of her car. They'd arrived just before the service was to begin.

Under one of her many Sunday-go-to-meeting hats, Glorieta nodded in approval. "Very picturesque." Mama G had a style all her own, a flair for life.

A tiny footbridge, spanning the small creek, connected the parking area to the church lawn. Rushing water burbled over the moss-covered stones. The apple-green leaves of a willow rustled in a light breeze.

Exactly as Kara remembered.

Arm in arm, she and Glorieta strolled over the footbridge. Church members had gathered on the steps of the sanctuary. Including the Double Name trifecta. Above the soft murmur of voices were sweet sounds of birdsong.

She recognized many who'd visited her café yesterday. The cowboy rancher and his rather elegant young wife, AnnaBeth. The attractive, curly redheaded woman in the flowing skirt, Lila, with her extremely handsome, blond fiancé. The police chief, although not in uniform today, and his wife, Maggie, who'd come yesterday with their twin boys.

Cute little Maddox must be about their sons' age. She didn't see any children. But perhaps there was a children's service in the adjacent educational building.

GeorgeAnne went stiff at the sight of her, but the others welcomed them. ErmaJean abandoned her companions to usher them inside the two-hundred-year-old sanctuary.

Huge, hand-hewn beams soared above their heads. Prisms of light refracted beams of color through the stained-glass windows. She and Glorieta slipped into the blue-cushioned pew. ErmaJean slipped in behind them.

This was the first time since that long-ago Homecoming Sunday that Kara had sat in this sanctuary. Coming home. That was what it had felt like then. That was what it felt like now.

A few weeks after that Sunday, her father was killed in a construction accident. She and her mom lost touch with the Hicks family. But ever since, Kara had held the memory of the town, the church and the people in a special place in her heart.

Today she let the peace of the music and the words of Scripture wash over her like cleansing rain.

After the service Reverend Bryant shook her and Glorieta's hands. Everyone was welcoming and friendly. She met lots of people, who all expressed a desire to visit the café in the coming week.

ErmaJean insisted she and Glorieta come to her house for Sunday dinner. "My cooking isn't grand, though. I'm an ordinary cook. I'm almost embarrassed to serve two chefs my simple food."

Glorieta shook her head. "Simple food is best. I'm just a cook, too." She patted ErmaJean's arm. "I wanted Kara to have the training I never received, but what matters most is the love behind the food."

They followed ErmaJean past the Welcome to Truelove sign, clattered across the bridge and turned off Main onto a quiet street in the neighborhood behind the elementary school.

ErmaJean pulled up in the driveway next to a rambling bungalow. Kara parked on the street behind an SUV. A young family got out of the vehicle.

Two little ash-blonde girls, twins, raced up the driveway toward Miss ErmaJean. "Gigi!" they shouted.

ErmaJean gathered them close as the girls talked over each other in excitement about children's church that morning.

"Hi, I'm Ethan, ErmaJean's grandson." The young man hugged the heavily pregnant woman at his side. "Those rambunctious two are our girls, Lucy and Stella. And this is my wife, Amber."

She and Glorieta introduced themselves.

Amber rubbed small circles on her belly. "The twins need no introduction. Folks a mile away can tell when we're home."

Glorieta smiled. "Your children are lovely. You're doing a great job with them."

"Thank you. Sometimes it's nice to be reminded." Amber's sky-blue eyes watered. "I don't know why I'm so emotional."

"Pregnancy hormones." Glorieta took Amber's arm as

they walked up the driveway toward the house. "I remember them well. When are you due?"

"Next month, after Easter." She blew a strand of wheat-blond hair out of her eyes. "And it can't come quick enough for me."

Letting go of the girls, ErmaJean gave Amber a hug. "She's a trouper. Still working full-time at the pediatrician's office."

Ethan grinned. "And putting up with me."

Amber's eyes twinkled. "That's the tricky part."

He laughed, and they shared a look of such sweet tenderness Kara felt a lump form in her throat. Surrounded by her pots and pans, most of the time she stayed too busy honing her craft to be lonely. But seeing them reminded her of what she might be missing. Recalling secret dreams she kept close to her heart.

Because it was a lovely day, lunch was a casual affair on the patio between the house and Ethan's furniture restoration workshop.

ErmaJean and Glorieta seemed to hit it off, which pleased Kara no end. Soon after lunch, the girls became restless and moved away from the table to play badminton in the yard.

"You two seem so close." ErmaJean handed Kara a plate with a slice of pound cake. "How did you and Glorieta meet?"

Tensing, Kara accepted the plate from the old woman.

But Glorieta gave her a reassuring smile. "Actually, I fostered Kara after her mother passed."

And gave everyone the highly condensed version of events that led to Kara becoming part of the barbecue family dynasty. Skimming over the when, where and why of how they'd first met.

She didn't tell many people about that period of her

life. The memories of those years between Homecoming Sunday with her intact family and becoming part of the Ferguson clan were filled with such sadness that she preferred not to revisit them.

"I'm sorry to hear about what happened to your father, Kara." ErmaJean's face crumpled. "And your mother's illness, too. You were so young. How hard that must've been for you."

Kara pressed her lips together.

ErmaJean fretted her napkin. "Around here we believe family takes care of family. My late husband would've been grieved to know you had to go into the foster system. But we had no idea... I can't tell you how sorry I am."

Reaching over, she took the older lady's blue-veined hand. "The families lost touch. It happens."

"Yet, the Lord worked it for good." Mama G took hold of Kara's free hand. "And I got the daughter I never had but longed for."

"We know a little something about that, too, don't we baby cakes." Ethan kissed his wife's cheek. "Except in my case, a double heaping of blessing."

The twins, Lucy and Stella, were Amber's children from a brief, failed first marriage. Just then, the shuttle birdie sailed across the patio and landed smack in the middle of the table. Resting like a plastic white crown atop the pound cake.

"Sorry!" seven-year-old Lucy called.

But the interruption served to divert the conversation toward less emotionally charged topics. Ethan tossed the birdie back to the twins.

ErmaJean gave them an earful on the latest Truelove happenings. Including the proposed shutdown of the fire station.

"That's terrible," Glorieta murmured.

If Will lost his job, would he and Maddox move away? The idea pained Kara. For Maddox's sake, of course.

"Will's my neighbor. Lives across the street." Erma-Jean lifted the tea pitcher. "Can I get anyone more tea?"

"Please. And thank you." Glorieta held out her glass. "Did we meet him at church this morning, Kara?"

"No, I didn't see him."

And yes, she'd looked.

"Maddox went to children's church with his grandfather today, but Will hasn't been to church since they returned to Truelove." ErmaJean's mouth pursed. "Not since his wife—"

"Grandma." Ethan settled his shoulders against the back of the chair. "No use in raking up the past. What's done is done."

Nothing further was said about the fire chief. The conversation moved on to other community events. Like the upcoming pancake fund-raiser and Easter celebrations. It appeared ErmaJean was on every committee in Truelove.

Kara enjoyed getting to know Amber and Ethan. For some inexplicable reason, their teasing, playful relationship reminded her of Will. Not that she had a relationship with Will. They were merely acquaintances.

Given time, could they become friends? Although with the potential closure of the fire station, the opportunity might never arise.

Long-term, she wanted what most women wanted—a husband, children, a lovely home and maybe a dog. She held on to the hope that after the restaurant was firmly established, she'd have more free time to pursue a personal life.

"I'd love to get together with you, Kara." Amber opened her arms as one of the twins—the quieter one, Stella—deposited herself in her mother's lap. "And introduce you to some other women our age, like my best friend, Callie. Her family owns an apple orchard."

"I'd like that." Up till now, ErmaJean had been her only friend in Truelove. "Thank you."

"The welcome sign doesn't lie." Glorieta beamed. "Truelove's reputation is well deserved, I'm glad to see. My Kara is in good hands here."

Amber winked at her husband. "And not just the first part on the sign, either."

"Truelove—where true love awaits." Grinning, he nudged his grandmother. "Thanks to a little help from certain friends."

"Love isn't only for the young, but also for the young at heart." ErmaJean wagged her finger. "You stick around long enough, Glorieta Ferguson, and you might find your one true love, too."

At Mama G's expression, Kara nearly choked on her sweet tea.

"No one's ever too old for love." Amber turned to her husband. "How many from the older generation is it now?"

"Your father and Deirdre." Ethan counted off on his fingers. "Callie's dad and Lorena. Tom Arledge and Wilda."

A Cheshire cat grin lifting her plump cheeks, ErmaJean steepled her hands. "Love might find you, too, Glorieta."

The barbecue queen's mouth went prim. "And just you remember, ErmaJean Hicks, that what goes around eventually comes around."

ErmaJean reared. "Me?"

"Yeah, Grandma." Ethan made room for Lucy as she crawled into his lap. "Wouldn't that be a hoot?"

With reluctance, Kara rose. "I hate to call it a day, but I have to get the dough prepared for baking tomorrow morning."

"Oh, must you go already?" ErmaJean's face fell. "I was hoping to trade recipes with Glorieta."

"Thank you so much for inviting me to lunch, Miss ErmaJean." Kara caught her foster mom's eye. "Mama G, you should really get on the road."

She'd put it off as long as she could. Dreading the moment Mama G went back to Durham. But she didn't want the older woman driving home in the dark.

"I've decided to stay in Truelove another week." Glorieta didn't stir from her chair. "If that's okay with you, Kara Lynn?"

Kara blinked. "I'd love to have you here, but aren't you needed back home?"

"My boys don't need me looking over their shoulder. Besides—" Glorieta fluttered her hand "—I'm enjoying the clean mountain air, and ErmaJean's invited me to become an honorary member of the Double Name Club. Hug me before you go. ErmaJean and I are going to talk turkey."

Kara hugged the stout older woman. "How will you get back to the motel?"

"GeorgeAnne's called a Citizens Concerned For Truelove meeting about something or other. I'll drop Glorieta off on my way." Rising, ErmaJean embraced Kara. The older lady smelled of cinnamon. "I hope this is the first of many social occasions in the future between our families, dear heart."

The twins were drooping. Amber and Ethan said their goodbyes, and took the girls inside for some quiet time.

Leaving ErmaJean and Glorieta to debate the best way to cook a Thanksgiving turkey, Kara waved goodbye.

Smiling, she made her way around the corner of the bungalow. Walking down the driveway to her car, her gaze drifted across the street to the well-kept, two-story house with the Dutch gambrel roof.

The fire chief's white SUV sat in the driveway next to what she guessed were their personal vehicles—a black pickup truck and a green Subaru.

Chewing her lip, she got in her car. There was something she was missing about Maddox's mother, but she didn't know what. And she didn't want to ask. She'd prefer Will tell her himself. If he wanted to.

He was a great guy. A wonderful father. She sensed he'd make a good friend. Though the likelihood of that happening with his precarious job situation was not looking good.

And the idea of not getting to know him depressed her more than it should. More than seemed reasonable for their limited acquaintance. But it made her sad she might never get the chance to know him better.

Pulling away finally from the curb, she steered the car down the street and headed toward the café.

Because as always, the best remedy for dealing with her loneliness was to get back into her safe haven, her refuge, her domain—the kitchen.

Chapter Four

Sunday afternoon found Will, his dad and Maddox relaxing on the screened porch off the backyard. At least, Will and Pops were trying to relax. Maddox had an agenda.

"De kitty cat could be hungwy or firsty, Daddy."

Ready for a nap, Will settled deeper into the cushions on the swing. "I'm sure Miss Kara will make sure the cat doesn't go hungry or thirsty."

"But she isn't dere on Sundays."

Will closed his eyes. A few blessed ticks of silence. Then—

"De kitty is lonely, Daddy. De kitty misses me."

More silence followed. And just when he thought himself home free—

"Don't you miss me when I'm not here, Daddy?"

From the wicker settee, Pops chuckled. "Got you there."

Will opened his eyes.

Maddox bounced on the tips of his shoes. "Pwease. Pwease, can we go see de kitty?"

He had seldom seen Maddox so passionate. An animal lover, his son had been begging for a pet for his next birthday. Not a good idea with their future so uncertain. But if a quick visit to the stray might temporarily pacify Maddox...

With a resigned sigh, Will swung his legs off the swing and stood up. "All right. Let's go."

He helped Maddox climb into his booster seat in the truck. He pulled out of the driveway, noting Kara's car was no longer parked at the curb across the street outside ErmaJean's house.

While waiting for Maddox and Pops to return from church, he'd seen her and the older African American lady arrive with Ethan's family for lunch. Miss ErmaJean was no slouch in the kitchen. Whereas Will's favorite thing to make for dinner was reservations.

"Maybe Miss Karwa's at de café."

Palming the wheel, he veered out of their neighborhood. "Then we don't need to go feed the cat." He glanced in the rearview mirror.

Maddox's lip protruded. "I want to see de kitty. I want to see Miss Karwa."

He headed toward downtown. "Miss Kara's probably not at the Mason Jar."

She was probably at the house he'd heard she was renting from Wilda Arledge. He frowned. Yeah, curiosity killed the cat. But so what if he'd asked Pops? He wanted to know.

"I wike Miss Karwa." Maddox turned from his contemplation of the window. "Do you wike Miss Karwa, Daddy?"

His mouth went dry. He did. He liked her very much. Too much. And it scared him.

Best thing he could do was to steer clear of her as much as possible. Easier said than done. In a town the size of Truelove, not an easy feat.

Passing the empty school playground, Maddox perked in his seat. "I hope we see her."

A secret part of Will hoped so, too. Rounding the

square, he caught sight of the blue sedan parked in front of the restaurant. His breath hitched.

Looked like Maddox's hope was about to be realized. He parked beside her vehicle. Maybe running into her like this was for the best.

The petition thing had bothered him all night. He didn't like the idea of her being ambushed. That wasn't the way he operated. She deserved fair warning of what she was up against.

He shut off the ignition. So that was what he'd do. Give her a heads-up and then stay far, far away from her.

Pleased with his resolution, he climbed out. After collecting Maddox, they stepped up to the entrance. The front dining area looked dark. Déjà vu to their first encounter.

"Miss Kara could be busy."

"Not too busy for me. She wikes me, Daddy." Maddox waggled his eyebrows. "And if you'd stop fwowning at her, she'd wike you, too."

"I don't frown at her." He frowned.

"Pops says—" the little boy deepened his voice "—you need to turn dat fwown upside down, mister."

He bit back a smile. Maddox had done a fair imitation of his grandfather's gravelly tone. And yes, if Will had heard Pops say it once, he'd heard it a hundred times. Mom used to remark Will was too serious for his own good.

Maddox grabbed the door handle and pulled it open. The bell jangled. A light shone through the cut-out window from the kitchen.

"Hello?" Kara peered around the porthole door and flicked the light switch. "Oh." She tilted her head. "Hi. It's you."

She looked very professional in a white chef coat. And as irresistible as one of her chocolate éclairs. Suddenly shy, Maddox hung back against his side.

He frowned. "The entrance should be locked when you're here alone."

"So you and Mama G keep reminding me."

Maddox tugged at his jeans. "Upside down, Daddy."

She gave his son a quizzical look. "What?"

He swiped his hand over his face and relaxed his features. "Nothing." He cleared his throat.

"Was there a reason you stopped by?"

"Maddox wanted to see the cat."

"Daddy wanted to see you."

Flushing, he gaped at his son. Not entirely accurate. But close enough.

Lips twitching, her gaze ping-ponged between them. "So which is it?"

Both...

"Maddox was worried the cat would starve between Saturday afternoon and Monday morning." He rubbed the back of his neck. "We're probably keeping you from something."

"I'd just put the last tray of pastry dough in the freezer when I heard the bell. I prep as much as I can the afternoon before, so it's ready to pop into the oven the next morning." She went into a crouch beside Maddox. "What a kind heart you have, to think of Soufflé."

Will chuckled. "Soufflé?"

"The name seemed to suit his cream color." She smiled. "And the tabby loves my soufflé."

"You named the stray?" He scratched his head. "Next step, you'll be taking him home."

"Not with my schedule." She planted her hands on her hips. "No time for pets or much else."

He wondered if she had time for someone else. Was someone in her life? He clamped his jaw tight.

What was wrong with him? Her love life was none of

his business. What did it matter if she had someone in her life or not?

However, the idea of someone special unsettled him. Made him feel like the cat with its fur rubbed up the wrong way. He broadened his chest.

What was with her naming the stray Soufflé? What kind of name was that for a cat? But it did remind him of something else.

"About that apple thing on your menu…"

She brightened. "You've come for your rain check. The apple galette goes into the oven first thing Monday morning. You'll have to wait until then, I'm afraid. But I'll save you a piece."

Her dimples flashed. She smiled at him. A ray of pure sunshine. His pulse skyrocketed.

Feeling slightly gobsmacked, he completely lost his train of thought. When she smiled at him, he found it incredibly hard to think at all. He could get used to her smile. Too used to it.

He scowled. *Don't get used to it.*

"Sue-flay?" Maddox tried the syllables on his tongue. No longer bashful, he hugged Kara. "I wike Soufflé, but I wuv you, Miss Karwa."

Will's mouth dropped open.

Her expression tender, she brushed her cheek against Maddox's hair. "I love you, too, sweetie pie." Planting a quick kiss on his head, she rose. "How about let's check on Soufflé?"

Closing his mouth, Will unglued his feet from the linoleum and followed them into the kitchen.

Maddox gazed at the stainless-steel pots hanging above the prep counter. "I want to cook some-ding first."

Will shook his head. "Maddox—"

"I have just the thing." She threw Will a grin. "Quick. Easy. Fun. And yummy."

She headed into the pantry and returned with a box of vanilla wafers, a jar of peanut butter and a bag of small marshmallows in her arms. "My mother used to make this with me when I was a little girl."

Maddox's lips curved down. "I don't have a mommy."

Her smile fading, she darted a look at Will.

"Does your mommy live in Trwoo-wuv, Miss Karwa?"

She set the items on the steel countertop. "No, sweetie. My mom died of cancer when I was a little girl."

"I sowee, Miss Karwa. Pops had cancer, too. But he finished his medicine so he's getting better."

She put her arms around the child. "I'm so happy to hear that, sweet boy."

"My mom died when Maddox was a baby. Heart attack." Will pulled over a stool for his son. "I was with the Charlotte Fire Department then."

A vein pulsed in the small hollow of her throat where the top button of her white jacket was undone. "Never easy no matter how old you are."

They shared a long look of sympathy. And he found himself mesmerized by the blue ocean depth in her eyes. The connection between them was only broken when Maddox mounted the step stool and reached for the peanut butter.

Whirling into action, she grabbed a bar towel from a stack. "Let's put something over your clothes." She tied the cloth around his waist. They went to work.

"Cooking" consisted of the petite blonde chef showing Maddox how to spread a dab of peanut butter across the top of the wafers and then dot each one with a single mini marshmallow.

"Wook, Daddy!" Up to his wrists in peanut butter, Maddox grinned. "I'm a cooker."

He laughed. "Yes, you are. Although, it looks like you're eating more than is going on the tray."

"Food should be fun." She winked. "As every great cooker knows, a messy kitchen is a happy kitchen."

He grinned. "If you say so."

She inserted the small metal tray into the toaster oven. "This is kind of like s'mores without the bonfire."

"Which works well," he said, smirking. "Since we're inside a building."

"Thank you, Fire Chief MacKenzie, for that reminder." She gave him a look. "In case we were in danger of forgetting the obvious."

"Anything to help, Chef."

"We'll set the dial to broil." She rotated the knob on the toaster oven. "But really it's about melting the peanut butter until it's all gooey."

"I wuv gooey, Miss Karwa."

"And who doesn't?" Batting her big blue eyes, she opened her hands. "Right?"

His heartbeat ticked up a notch. *Wow. Did she have any idea of how cute she looked?* The peanut butter wasn't the only thing feeling gooey.

She motioned over Maddox. "I'll set the timer to about two minutes. But you keep watch through the glass window. We'll take out the tray when the marshmallow turns your favorite scorched color."

He scooted Maddox and the stool closer to the steel counter. Legs dangling and attention rapt, Maddox fixed his gaze on the marshmallow doing a slow burn.

Will put the lid on the peanut butter jar. "Let me help with cleanup."

She rinsed off the small butter knife in the sink. "I

didn't realize you'd lived in Charlotte. Me, too. I went to culinary school at Johnson & Wales."

"That's impressive." He closed the box of wafers. "Even a non-foodie like me has heard of its reputation. How long ago were you there?"

Returning with a wet dishcloth, she wiped the area free of crumbs and peanut butter. As they chatted, they discovered they'd both been in the city of Charlotte about the same time.

And he couldn't help but wonder how different his life might have been if instead of meeting Liz when he first arrived, he'd met the perky, sunny culinary student.

The timer dinged.

He peered through the see-through window. "Looking a little toasty there, Maddox." He raised his eyebrows. "As in, almost burned to a crisp."

She twisted the heat setting to Off. "Beauty is in the eye of the beholder, remember? Applies to food, too."

And in his opinion, a French-inspired chef. Who was kind to kitty cats and motherless little boys. Beautiful inside and out.

Grabbing potholders, she carefully removed the tray and set it on the counter. "Let them cool. Meanwhile…" She looked at Maddox's hands.

He steered his son toward the sink. "I'll help Peanut Butter Boy get spic-and-span."

Maddox giggled. Then with the wafers now cool, she declared it was time to taste test.

After eating two in a row, Maddox came up for air. "What do you fink, Daddy?"

"So delicious I want another one." He popped the entire wafer into his mouth. "My compliments to the chef and the cooker."

Kara tilted her head. "You know what the most handsome guys know how to do, Chief MacKenzie?"

"No, I don't." He rolled his tongue in his cheek. "Please, enlighten me. What do the most handsome guys know how to do, Chef Lockwood?"

She rested her hand on his son's head. "Cook."

He bit back a smile.

Maddox tugged on her jacket. "Can I feed Soufflé now?"

For the second time in as many days, the three of them carried the bowl of water and an egg dish out to the back alley.

"Soufflé!" Maddox called. "I bwought you some-ding yummy!"

A pink nose peeked around the bin.

"See, Daddy. Soufflé knows me. We're friends."

The little boy squatted on his heels beside the saucer to watch the tabby eat.

"You said that Mama G and I keep reminding you to lock the diner." Will leaned his shoulder against the exterior wall. "Who's Mama G?"

A bemused smile on her features, Kara kept her eyes trained on his son and the cat. "You mean the *café*."

Reminding him once more of the subject he needed to broach with her. He straightened.

"Mama G is Glorieta Ferguson, my foster mom." Her eyes flitted to him and away again. "She helped me at the opening yesterday."

The African American lady he'd thought was the owner.

"Your foster mom?" He glanced at his son, who was still oblivious to anything outside his new feline friend. "How old were you when you came to live with her?"

"Eleven."

"I'm sorry."

"Don't be. Mama G is the best." She sighed. "But I don't know that you ever get beyond missing your mom."

He blew out a breath. "That's what I worry about with Maddox."

Kara's gaze held a question, but he was thankful she didn't press him to explain.

The little boy wanting Kara to cook at his house and be Will's wife had hit him right between the eyes. His son finally giving voice to a deep-seated desire for a mommy. Like his best buddies, Austin and Logan Hollingsworth. But with the current drama over the fire station, not something Will had either the time or energy to focus upon.

"Mama G and her family were good to me. Still are."

He jerked out of his reverie.

"Making her proud and the café a success is my number-one priority."

Will understood priorities. Maddox was the most important person in his life. His top priority. He couldn't afford to lose sight of that. And that was the way it should be. Was meant to be. Even if sometimes he felt lonely.

How long before Miss ErmaJean and her matchmaking cohorts found a perfect match for Kara? The old women were determined to make Truelove like Noah's ark. As in, they came in pairs. A party he had no wish to join.

And yet, the notion of Kara paired off with someone rankled. Or just someone *else*?

Flustered, he felt an overwhelming need to leave. To get away from the pretty chef and the complicated feelings she elicited within him.

He folded his arms. "Maddox, we should go."

The cat jumped at his voice and bolted down the alley.

"Daddy!" Maddox glared. "You scared Soufflé."

He took hold of his son's shoulder. "Miss Kara has better things to do with the rest of her Sunday than hang out in an alley."

Punching in the code on the door, she gave him a curious look. They followed her into the kitchen.

He navigated his child through the swinging door and into the dining area. "We've troubled you enough."

She trailed after them. "It's been no bother."

Yanking open the entrance door, he set the bell aquiver. "Tell Miss Kara thank you and goodbye, son."

"Dank you, Miss Karwa."

She hugged the little boy. "You are so welcome, sweetie pie."

With his child in her arms, something stirred in his heart. And conversely, irrationally, also made him angry.

They'd been doing just fine until they met her. *Thank you very much.* Even if his cooking skills did leave a lot to be desired.

"Come on, Maddox." He held the door. "Let's go."

"The wafers." She straightened. "I'll box them for you to take home."

He frowned. "That's not—"

But she'd darted back into the kitchen.

He gritted his teeth. This had to stop. Before Maddox became too attached. Before he became too—

Will pulled Maddox out to the sidewalk.

"But, Daddy..." His son looked over his shoulder. "Miss Karwa's bwinging de..."

Will hustled him over to the truck, careful to keep hold of his hand. Sunday afternoons on Main were usually pretty quiet, but it looked like some meeting had just broken up over at the hardware store. Traffic had picked up.

"Maddox. Will. Wait." Clutching a small white takeout box, she raced outside. "You weren't going to leave without these, were you?"

His son pulled on his sleeve. "Wook, Daddy. Soufflé followed us."

Several vehicles whizzed by.

Will frowned at the box. "You really didn't have to do that."

She held the box out to him. "It was fun."

Maddox tugged his hand. "Soufflé wants me to go play wid him, Daddy."

Letting go of him, Will scraped his hand across his face. "No, I mean you really shouldn't have done that, Kara."

She blinked at him. "What?"

"Thank you for being kind to my son, but…" He squared his shoulders. "A word of advice."

Her gaze sharpened. "Advice about what?"

"Soufflé." Maddox raised his voice to be heard over the passing cars. "And me, Daddy." He inched off the sidewalk.

Will jutted his jaw. "I think if you want the diner to be a success, you should reconsider your menu."

Her chin lifted. "What are you talking about? I kept my prices in line with the previous owner's."

Maddox took a step away and then another.

Will locked eyes with her. "I'm talking about taking the apple pie off the menu and replacing it with some fancy apple substitute."

"The apple tart galette?" Her eyes narrowed. "Have you even tried my version before you passed judgment?"

He widened his stance. "I don't have to try it to know Truelove loves its apple pie." He raised his palms. "And don't shoot the messenger because I'm trying to give you a friendly warning."

Kara scowled at him. "You insult my food, and you call that being friendly?"

"… Soufflé… Me… On the square, Daddy…"

Will scowled back. "People around here don't take

kindly to highhanded flatlanders telling us what we should and shouldn't eat. Furthermore…"

To his immense irritation, he realized she'd stopped listening. Her attention snared by a blur of motion. In his peripheral vision, he saw it, too.

A streak of movement. A cream-colored tabby. And a small boy.

His boy.

Maddox's words registered at the same moment she threw the box down and raced into the street.

"Stop, Maddox!" she screamed. "Don't move! Stop!"

He turned at what she'd seen behind him. But his reaction was a split second too late. Maddox had chased the stray into the middle of the intersection.

Adrenaline pumping, Will sprinted forward, but it felt as if his feet were encased in quicksand. And he knew. Somehow he just knew. He'd never reach Maddox in time.

Darting between the cars, she scooped his child into her arms.

Horns blared. There was a hissing squeal of brakes. Cars in both lanes skidded.

And then a horrific thud.

Chapter Five

Without stopping to think, Kara rushed into the street, determined to save Maddox from harm.

Grabbing up the little boy, she turned her back on the oncoming car. Using her body to shield him from the impact of a collision she knew was coming. She tensed. Flinched at the squeal of brakes. The hissing of braking tires.

Her eyes squeezed shut, it took her a few seconds to realize she was still alive. Her heart pounded.

On the back of her legs, she could feel the heat coming off the too-close engine. She waited for the onset of pain. A twinge. But nothing.

Vaguely, she became aware of voices shouting. One of them Will's. But all that mattered was Maddox. Was he okay?

Her eyes snapped open as Will wrenched the little boy from her arms.

"Are you all right, Maddox? Talk to me, son." Will examined the child from head to toe. "You know you're never supposed to go into the street without…" His gaze shot to her. "You saved him. Are you hurt, Kara?"

She couldn't speak past the boulder lodged in her throat.

His brow creased. "Darlin'?" His hand cradled her cheek, igniting sparks along her skin.

And her knees went weak at the drawled-out rasp of his voice.

He must have felt the sparks, too, because his dark eyes widened. But she didn't pull away. Neither did he.

Snarled in both directions, traffic came to a standstill. Motorists got out of their vehicles.

"Are they okay, Chief?"

"They ran right out in front of my car, Chief."

Holding Maddox against him and with an arm curled protectively around Kara's shoulders, Will took charge in sorting out the confusion.

The buzz of voices droned on around her. She felt strange. Numb, almost disconnected from reality. Probably in shock. If only she could stop shaking.

"Give yourself a second," Will said. "It's the excess adrenaline leaving your system."

Suddenly, Maddox caught sight of something over Will's shoulder. "Soufflé's hurt!" Squirming, he tried climbing down from his father's arms. "He's not dead, is he, Daddy?"

They both turned to find the little stray cat lying motionless near the curb.

"No. No. No," Maddox sobbed. "Please, Daddy. Make him get up."

Setting his son on his feet, Will's face went grim. "Kara, could you take Maddox while I check Soufflé?" He gripped the little boy's shoulders to prevent him from dashing over.

Pulling herself together, Kara held out her arms. "Let me hold you, sweetie pie."

The little boy strained away from her.

"Sweetheart, please." Snapped out of her shock, she

lifted the struggling child. "Let Daddy look at Soufflé first."

Crying, Maddox buried his face into her chest. Her arms wrapped around him, she could feel his little body quivering. She brought the little boy to the sidewalk.

"No signs of bleeding." Crouching, Will's gaze roamed over the inert cat. "His eyes are open, and he's breathing."

She gave Maddox a quick squeeze. "Did you hear what Daddy said? Soufflé is still alive."

The little boy lifted his head. "Soufflé's not dead, Daddy?"

"No, son." Will glanced from the cat to the large sedan. "But it looks like he was hit by the car."

Her lips trembled. "Run over?"

Will shook his head. "I don't think so. Maybe just knocked for a loop and bounced over to the curb."

Abruptly, the cat staggered to its feet, only to collapse again.

Will rose. "I'm going to immobilize Soufflé in my jacket so he doesn't further injure himself. We need to take him to the vet." He gestured at the veterinary clinic several blocks away on Main.

Maddox slid out of Kara's embrace. "Firefighters help ever-wee-body, Miss Karwa." He smiled. "Daddy will make Soufflé all better."

She and Will exchanged an anxious look.

Oh, Lord, please help us help the tabby.

She hugged the little boy at her side. "I'm sure Daddy and the veterinarian will do their best."

Will gently lifted the cat a few inches off the asphalt. She and Maddox spread the navy blue TFD jacket underneath the injured stray.

"Uh, Kara. I hate to ask this of you… But I don't think it's a good idea for Maddox to hold the cat while I drive."

He was right. There was no telling how the injured animal might respond to handling. The cat could strike out while in pain and hurt Maddox.

"You don't have to ask." She raised her chin. "Of course, I'm coming with you and Maddox."

"And Soufflé," Maddox piped.

She nodded. "And Soufflé. But first, can you help me lock up the restaurant, Maddox?"

Carrying him inside, she put him in charge of turning off all the lights. A minute later they stood outside once more, and she turned the key, locking the entrance behind them.

The crowd and vehicles had dispersed. And Will, with the tabby in his arms, waited for them beside his black truck.

"I put in a call to the clinic. The vet is waiting for us." He looked at Kara. "I think it would be a good idea for you to drive."

She blinked. "You trust me to drive your vehicle?"

He locked gazes with her. "If I can trust you to save the life of my son, I think I can trust you to drive my truck." His voice softened. "And thank you for that, by the way." His Adam's apple bobbed in his throat. "So much," he rasped.

In that instant something passed between them. Leaving her slightly breathless and wanting more.

Kara picked up Maddox, holding him on her hip. His little arms went around her neck. She kissed his cheek and glanced from father to son.

Please, Lord. Yes. So much more.

The journey from the Mason Jar to the vet clinic was mercifully brief. Sitting on the passenger side, Will cradled the cat in his arms. The tabby had been remarkably compliant, as if sensing they were trying to help him.

Behind the wheel of his big truck, Kara seemed somehow even more tiny. But she'd been steady of mind and large of heart throughout the whole ordeal.

The female vet on call this weekend, also new to Truelove, met them at the door. There was an antiseptic smell to the clinic. He carefully placed the cat, wrapped like a mummy in the folds of his jacket, on the small gurney.

Holding Maddox's hand, he and Kara stood back to allow the vet to do a preliminary evaluation. He'd had no reason to meet the veterinarian before now. She was strikingly attractive with a brisk, competent air. And she was tall.

Though in his opinion, tall women were overrated. Liz had been tall.

"It's a good thing you brought him in when you did, Chief MacKenzie."

No surprise she knew who he was. Such was small-town life. And the infamous Truelove grapevine.

"From your description of the accident, I'm thinking we could be dealing with a blunt force head trauma."

They kept quiet as the vet listened to Soufflé's chest and lungs.

Dr. Abernathy straightened, letting the stethoscope drape around the collar of her lab coat. "I'll know more once I've conducted a full examination."

"Soufflé couldn't walk, Dr. 'Naffy," Maddox interjected.

The vet, about Will's age, gave the little boy a slight smile. "Soufflé?" Her blue eyes flicked to Kara. "Although, what else would a chef name a cat, right?"

Kara bit her lip. "He appeared to be in some pain, too, Dr. Abernathy."

"Why don't y'all take a seat in the reception area?"

The woman reached to pat Maddox's head. But Maddox jerked away from her touch. Fairly typical from Will's not-too-keen-on-strangers son. As for Maddox's attachment to Kara? That was an anomaly Will had no explanation for.

With far too many hospital stays in the short space of his life, maybe it was simply a matter of the well-earned, white coat aversion Maddox had acquired for medical personnel.

Dr. Abernathy gave his son a quizzical look. "I can always call with the results if your son needs his nap."

"I'm fwee." Scowling, Maddox held up three fingers. "Naps awe for babies."

Will put his hand on his son's shoulder. "We'll wait." He hoped the vet was better with animals than she was with small boys.

The vet's blue-eyed gaze flitted to Kara. "All of you?" Her eyebrow arched.

Kara rested her hand on Maddox's short brown hair. "All of us."

With a steely smile, the vet wheeled the gurney through a double set of doors.

He led his son and Kara over to the waiting area and a pair of upholstered chairs. Sitting, he opened his arms, but instead, Maddox climbed into Kara's lap.

Apparently, white chef coats were another matter entirely from lab coats.

Maddox tucked himself under Kara's chin. Within seconds Will detected the soft, even sound of his breathing.

"He's fallen asleep," she whispered.

"Obviously, very much in need of a nap." Will rolled his eyes. "I have no idea what his deal was with the vet, though."

Kara hitched her eyebrow. "She offended his three-year-old pride."

Will's lips curved. "She didn't seem all that good with humans in general."

Kara nudged him with her elbow. "She seemed to like fire chiefs well enough."

"Thanks, but no, thanks." He fidgeted. "Reminds me too much of Liz."

Kara's lips parted. He'd surprised her, but to her credit, she didn't pry. Which made him admire her all the more.

"Although, when it comes to firefighters…" He threw her a cocky grin. "What's not to like?"

She rolled her eyes. "What's so sad is that you actually think you're funny."

He laughed. Maddox stirred.

"Shh…" She resettled Maddox in her lap.

"If your arms are tired, I can—"

Kara shied away. "My arms never get too tired of holding Maddox."

He sighed. "It's a shame his own mother didn't feel the same."

She went motionless.

In for a penny, in for a pound. He'd bottled his feelings too long. If he was going to unburden himself to anyone, and he wasn't sure why, he wanted it to be her.

"My parents never liked her." Will raked his hand over his head. "That should've been my first clue. But when it came to Liz, I was basically clueless."

"You were in love with her," Kara whispered. She wasn't sure why she was whispering.

He grimaced. "I was certainly besotted with her. I realize now what Liz and I shared had very little to do with love." His shoulders slumped. "Not the kind of love that lasts."

Kara held herself still, afraid to breathe, unsure how to respond.

"My parents taught me right from wrong, but after I went to the firefighter academy…" He lowered his gaze, unable to meet her eyes. "Liz wasn't like the girls I'd known in Truelove. She lived for the next party and didn't believe the rules applied to us." He swallowed. "But as I learned the hard way, consequences did."

Kara took a quick breath. "You don't have to—"

"I want you to know."

His brown eyes bored into Kara. Searching her face. Trying to gauge her reaction. Probing for something. What, though?

"I messed up. Big time. Got things with her totally out of order. I was an idiot."

"You were young."

"I was old enough to know better," he grunted.

"You're not the same man now."

His mouth pursed. "How can you tell?"

She lifted her chin. "Because of the little guy I'm holding in my arms."

He looked at her. A long, long moment. "Thank you, Kara," he rasped. "Thank you for saying that."

"You're welcome." She brushed her cheek against the silk of his son's hair. "And no matter whatever else happened, you gave life to this precious, precious child."

Hands gripping his knees, he leaned back in the chair. "You make it sound far easier than it was. I wanted to do right by her. To live up to my responsibilities. But first, I had to convince her to keep the baby."

Kara stiffened.

"Which was almost as hard as convincing her we should get married." He laughed, but it was a sound without mirth.

"She hated being pregnant because of the changes to her body. She hated being married because it tied her down."

Kara touched his forearm, the muscles sinewy below the rolled-up sleeves of his button-down shirt. "I'm so sorry."

Her fingertips tingled from the touch of his skin. His dark eyes darkened even further. Before she could withdraw her hand, his palm covered hers, holding it on his arm. Her heartbeat accelerated.

She became transfixed at the patch of skin in the hollow at the base of his throat above his open collar where a vein pulsed.

All of a sudden he pulled back, and his eyes became hooded. "Maddox was born premature with serious health issues, and Liz refused to even hold him. He had his first surgery when he was two days old." Will raised his gaze to Kara. "That's the same day Liz left the hospital and never came back. She couldn't wait to be rid of us both."

Kara went rigid. "She walked out on you while her two-day-old son was in surgery?"

"She relinquished all parental rights to Maddox, and the divorce was handled through our lawyers."

The look of utter failure on his face made her heart hurt. "Neither of you deserved that."

Dr. Abernathy returned to the waiting room. They stood up. Maddox rubbed his eyes.

"I suspect Soufflé suffered a closed head injury, but thankfully mild. It could take a few weeks for Soufflé's brain to fully heal from the concussion."

Will's forehead creased. "Cats get concussions?"

"It's more common than you'd believe." Dr. Abernathy stuck her hands into her lab coat pockets. "Soufflé has also suffered a Grade 1 sprain on his left foreleg."

Kara winced. "That sounds painful."

"I've splinted the leg. And I gave him an anti-inflammatory

medication to reduce swelling in the limb to speed healing and alleviate any pain. He will need to be restricted to his cage so he can rest and allow the limb to regain normal function."

Kara gnawed her bottom lip. "But Soufflé is an outdoor cat."

The veterinarian shrugged. "As long as the splint is in place, he must be confined indoors and not allowed to roam for fear of worsening the injury. A resting regimen must be strictly enforced for at least two weeks."

Kara shook her head. "Soufflé is a stray."

Dr. Abernathy's lips thinned. "A stray? I thought the cat belonged to you, Miss Lockwood. Strays don't usually have names. Who's going to be responsible for the medical costs today?" She glanced between them.

Kara drooped. "I—I—"

"I'll be taking care of the cost, Dr. Abernathy." Will took Maddox out of Kara's arms. "I guess I'll need to pick up a crate at the pet store and supplies."

"No, Will." Kara knotted her hands. "This isn't your responsibility."

"I insist." He adjusted his son's weight on his arm. "If Maddox hadn't chased him…"

"Soufflé would've still run into the road." She shook her head. "If you insist on paying the veterinarian bill, then I insist on taking Soufflé home and overseeing his recovery."

"You've got a restaurant to run."

Dr. Abernathy crossed her arms. "During his recovery, Soufflé can board here at the clinic for an additional cost."

Kara frowned. "And after he's healed, what would happen to him then?"

"Seeing as the cat doesn't belong to anyone, I'd turn him over to a cat rescue facility to find him a forever home."

Kara bit her lip. "But what if no one comes forward to adopt him?"

"Then he'll live out his life there. It's a no-kill shelter."

Her heart pounded. A shelter for cats with no place or no one to call their own. Abandoned. Forgotten. A dumping ground for society's unwanted?

All of which hit far too close for comfort.

She took a deep breath. "I'll take him home with me."

"Are you sure?" He shifted Maddox to his other arm. "How will you juggle the restaurant and Soufflé?"

She squared her shoulders. "I'll make it work."

Maddox fidgeted and Will put him down. "I help take care of Soufflé, Miss Karwa. Ever-wee-day." He tugged at her white coat. "Pwease. Pwease."

She shot a glance at Will. "That's totally up to your dad, sweetie pie."

Will stuck his hands in his jeans. "Miss Kara might get sick of seeing us every day."

"I won't."

"Can I help Miss Karwa, Daddy? Can I?" A human pogo stick, he bounced from his father to Kara and back again. "I'll be de best helper you ever saw, Miss Karwa. Pwease, Daddy?"

"Since Miss Kara doesn't mind, I see no reason why I should, either."

Maddox fist-pumped the air. "Yay! Yay! Hoo-ray!"

Will headed toward the reception desk to settle the bill. And somehow he managed to sweet-talk the vet into allowing them the loan of a cage.

Dr. Abernathy ran his payment through the credit card machine. "Oddly enough for a stray, Soufflé was already neutered. Probably when he was a kitten."

Kara planted her hands on her hips. "And then his owner

just abandoned him? Turned him out when he wasn't cute and cuddly anymore?"

Will and the vet glanced at her. Kara flushed.

"I'll need to see Soufflé for a follow-up visit in about two weeks." The vet handed Will his receipt and a print-out of essential cat supplies. "And if I were you, I'd plan on giving the tabby a much-needed bath while he's still groggy from the medication."

On her cell, Kara searched for the closest pet store still open on a Sunday evening. "I'll call next week to make the appointment."

Will followed the vet into the back to load Soufflé into his new, temporary quarters. When he returned, Maddox murmured sweet words of encouragement and sympathy through the cage bars.

After a quick run to a big-box pet store in the new shopping center on the interstate, Kara found herself the proud new owner of several bags of special protein-enriched cat food, a few fun toys Maddox insisted Soufflé couldn't live without and a litter box.

She didn't consider herself Soufflé's owner. She might not know much about independent felines, but one thing she did know—nobody owned a cat. In fact, it was probably the other way around. From day one it would seem it was Soufflé who'd claimed Kara as his own.

Coming out of the store, Maddox declared himself to be starving. She volunteered to make dinner at her house, but Will refused.

"You've saved my son and given a cat a home." He grinned, exposing even white teeth.

Be still my heart. That smile really ought to come with a warning label. As in, potential to cause heart palpitations.

He turned into a burger drive-through. "I think I can swing dinner."

"Surely, my food is better than this burger joint."

"Absolutely." He waited behind another vehicle to order. "But there's nothing wrong with an occasional burger. Not too hot. Not too cold. Just right."

Moments later he pulled away, and she unpacked the takeout bag. Laying his cheeseburger on the seat between them, she made a face.

He laughed at her turned-up nose. "Not every meal has to be haute cuisine, Goldilocks."

"You have the taste buds of a Neanderthal, Papa Bear."

They grinned at each other across the truck cab.

"You're very pretty for a food snob."

Tucking a strand of hair behind her ear, she blushed. *He thinks I'm pretty?* Maddox slurped his shake from his booster seat. Soufflé meowed from the back.

One-handing the wheel, Will bit into a french fry. "You can rain check me on the home-cooked dinner."

"The rain checks are starting to pile up."

He flicked his eyes at her. "No worries. I aim to collect on each and every one."

She felt hot, then cold. And finally, just right.

He carried the crate with Soufflé into her house. The tabby had taken the truck ride and shopping expedition in stride. She took Dr. Abernathy's suggestion regarding a bath to heart. With Maddox and Will's help, it went better than she'd expected.

Back inside the crate with his fur returned to its original cream luster, Soufflé calmly contemplated his new domain.

Will gathered his son into his arms. "Let me check with Pops first, but we'll work out a time for Maddox to look in on Soufflé tomorrow."

"Sounds good."

With his child visibly wilting from fatigue, Will bid her good-night.

She watched out the window until his red taillights disappeared out of sight around the corner. It had been a very good day. Sunday service with Glorieta. And time spent with a certain handsome fire chief and his adorable son.

After his surprising disclosure about Maddox's mother, somehow she felt they'd moved from acquaintances to something more.

"We're just friends," she told Soufflé as she got into bed that night.

Inside the crate on the floor, the tabby's green eyes did a slow blink.

"Which is entirely as it should be." She flopped against the pillow. "Because I have a restaurant to run, and he needs to save his job."

Soufflé yawned, his jaws stretching wide.

"No, seriously." She switched off the bedside lamp. "We're nothing more than friends."

It was only just before she drifted to sleep, she remembered Will had called her *darlin'*.

Chapter Six

Will lay awake half the night sifting through Kara's reaction to his revelation about his ex-wife.

Sometimes he felt like such a failure in the relationship department. Yet, there'd been no condemnation in her eyes, only empathy. And something else he wasn't ready to put a name to, but which teased at the fringes of his mind all night.

Over the next several days Maddox and Pops worked out a system with Kara to check on Soufflé during the day while she was at the diner. Will got into the habit of taking a coffee break midafternoon just before she closed the restaurant each day.

Glorieta introduced herself to him. It was only later, after a word with ErmaJean, that he realized Kara's foster mom was also *the* Glorieta Ferguson of Mama G restaurant fame.

The barbecue queen watched as Kara presented a slice of birthday cake topped with a lit candle to Mrs. Desmond, who lived near Miss IdaLee. "That girl of mine gives her love by feeding people."

He pretended not to notice the lonely widow had her Chihuahua tucked into her leather tote.

"Kara's waving me over. I'd best go say hello." Glorieta climbed off the adjacent stool. "We may not look a lot alike on the outside, but inside, our hearts look the same."

He enjoyed watching the dynamic between Kara and her foster mom. Glorieta could be a real firecracker at times. He could readily see where the petite chef got her sass and her spark.

Most of all, he enjoyed getting to know Kara better. They were opposites in many areas, but not so much in the things that really mattered like their commitment to family.

Of course, Maddox had been head over heels smitten since the beginning. And Pops wasn't far behind in his praise of Kara. Will noticed his father was spending a lot of time at the diner these days.

He wasn't sure if the draw was Kara, the food or perhaps her foster mom. More afternoons than not, he'd arrive to find his dad and the inimitable barbecue queen in the corner booth swapping I-remember-when stories and chuckling.

Will spent the majority of his week prepping for the all-important council meeting, whose main agenda item was the proposed closure of the Truelove firehouse. His crew was anxious about the outcome. So was he.

Thursday morning outside the town hall, he waited for Truelove's chief of police, Bridger Hollingsworth, to join him before heading inside to face the council.

Ambling over from the police station, Bridger threw up his hand when he spotted Will on the sidewalk. They were about the same age, and since they'd both taken their current positions about the same time a year ago, had become friends.

Their jobs made them both serious by nature. They were both dedicated to public service. And they both had sons. Bridger's three-year-old twins, Austin and Logan, were

Maddox's best friends. But there the similarities ended. The police chief was happily married to Maggie, a fitness instructor at the rec center. Whereas Will was not-so-happily single.

Whoa. Since when had he become unhappy about his singleness? He had a sneaking suspicion it was about the time he met Kara.

He extended his hand to Bridger. "Thanks for coming today. Your support could convince some of the council members to reconsider closing the station."

An imposing man with dark hair and intense blue eyes, Bridger shook his hand. "I don't know how much help I'll be. In the current economic climate, I understand the need for budget cuts, but I can't believe the council is proposing to entirely dismantle the TFD."

Will held the door as they entered the lobby. "With the larger county fire station, many of the council members see it as a way to reduce what they perceive as a redundancy of services."

Bridger removed his head cover. "They don't realize that the loss of the station will make for longer response times. And put lives at risk."

Skipping the elevator, they took the winding marble steps to the second floor council chamber.

Will paused at the top of the stairs. "How's the class going? Maggie okay?"

Currently, Bridger and Maggie were co-teaching a self-defense class, a subject near and dear to their hearts, to the women of Truelove. Years earlier Maggie had survived a traumatic assault. But it had left emotional scars.

At the mention of his wife, Bridger's face lit up. "The class is going well. An important part of the healing process for her. And thanks for asking. She's good. We're good." The police chief grinned. "Better than good. We're great."

For the first time since Liz walked away, Will wanted that, too, for himself. However, until just this moment, he hadn't believed it possible that he could move past the bitterness. Until he met Kara?

The meeting lasted over two hours. With the members unable to reach a consensus and with the session becoming increasingly heated, Mayor Watson called for an adjournment. He proposed to table the discussion until the next meeting in one week's time.

Outside again, Will and Bridger parted company.

"Don't give up yet. We've plenty more fight left in us." Bridger touched his shoulder. "I hear Maddox is spending the morning with Austin and Logan."

"He loves the three-year-old ninja warrior class that Maggie teaches. He's also looking forward to their lunch playdate afterward." Will sighed. "I never wanted him to grow up an only child like me. Just one more thing to feel guilty about."

"Maddox is a great kid." Bridger rested his hands on his gun belt. "And who's to say he'll always be an only child?" The lawman's mouth curved. "Maddox has been telling my boys how much he and Daddy love cooking something up with a certain blonde chef."

"I…" Will sputtered. "She's been kind to my son. And Maddox has developed a sudden interest in this stray cat Kara is fostering."

Bridger laughed. "And what has Maddox's father developed a sudden interest in?"

Will toed the sidewalk with his shoe. "There's absolutely nothing going on between Kara Lockwood and me. Even if I wanted to—which I don't—I have no time." He scrubbed his mouth with his hand. "Especially not now with everything up in the air about the department."

Bridger raised his hands, palms up. "If that's your story, stick with it by all means." His chest rumbled. "But it's like my mom always says, 'the bit dog always barks the loudest.'" He grinned. "And since sooner or later the matchmakers are sure to home in on this very interesting nonrelationship you have with Kara, assuming they haven't already…"

Will scoured his hand over his face.

"You might want to consult with me for tips on body language before they get around to asking you about your feelings for the aforementioned chef."

Will grimaced. "Glad to know you find my private life so entertaining."

"Hey, don't knock it till you've tried it." The lawman stuck his tongue in his cheek. "I've lost count of how many successful marriages those three women have wrangled at this point. The matchmakers know a thing or two about the romance department."

Will rolled his eyes. "The matchmakers are a public menace. And right now I'm more concerned about another department. The Truelove Fire Department."

"I have a feeling the Double Name Club might be coming for you, buddy. Been there. Done that. And I've never been happier." Chuckling, the police chief headed back to his office.

Kara and the matchmakers were a distraction he didn't need in his life. What was he going to do if he lost his job?

Struggling to get his fears and emotions under control before he faced his crew at the station, he took the long way around the square and sank down on the steps of the gazebo to reflect on what he could have said differently at the meeting. On what his next move should be to protect firefighter jobs. His own, included.

The fire department had a strong ally in the mayor, but his was only one vote. GeorgeAnne wasn't wrong about flatlander newcomers and the changes they'd wrought on Truelove.

In his experience, change rarely brought anything good.

Gazing beyond the river toward the distant Blue Ridge vista surrounding the small Appalachian community, he felt his jagged, raw emotions begin to soothe. The mountains defined the citizens of Truelove. Defined him, too. Tough. Resilient.

He'd take country over city, mountain over flatland, any day of the week. Of course, he'd had to learn that lesson the hard way. But he'd had his fill of the noise, the anonymity of city living and the traffic.

Returning to Truelove had been about choosing a slower pace. Rediscovering neighborliness. Embracing the simplicity and goodness of small-town life.

Like him, the vast majority of sky-country natives, no matter how far or how long they roamed, eventually found their way back to the land of their birth. Somehow, it felt easier to breathe here.

And if it took a fight to preserve the TFD, then a fight was what the town council would get. He wasn't ready to give up on this town or the future he hoped to build with his son here. A future that might include a certain gorgeous Francophile chef?

To be determined. But he was smiling as he got off the steps and wended his way to the firehouse.

He should've known the quiet wouldn't last. The call came just after eleven thirty. One of those calls firefighters never forgot, but wished they could.

Several hours later he drove the SUV back to the station and got out. The big truck rolled up to the firehouse, stopping outside the apparatus bay.

After removing his helmet, he swiped his brow, face, jaw and neck with a hand wipe. Grim and disheartened, faces blackened with smoke, the men climbed down from the rig and removed their turnout gear.

His lieutenant, Bradley, wiped the inside of his helmet. "That was a bad one, Chief."

Most of Will's duties involved administration and training. It was mainly a nine-to-five weekday job. But even if he was off duty, he was called out to bigger fires.

Sometimes he missed being on the front lines. The action, the adrenaline, the camaraderie of teamwork. And the satisfaction of making a difference.

Today there'd been action, adrenaline and teamwork, but no satisfaction. Despite responding within minutes of getting the call, they'd not been able to get to the elderly couple in time.

Fire engine driver, Luke Morgan, stuffed his gear inside a plastic storage bag for washing. "I hate space heaters."

"We did everything we could to save them."

Luke, a young Christmas tree farmer, toed out of his boots. "It wasn't enough, though, was it?"

It was the early spring or fall when Will saw the most fallout from improper use of space heaters. The device had overheated. And less than a foot away, the curtain got too hot, catching fire. In mere minutes, the flames had jumped to the mattress, sending out choking black smoke. The couple hadn't stood a chance.

He removed his turnout coat. The next shift was due to arrive soon. As the crew cleaned the equipment, he went from firefighter to firefighter, offering encouragement. It was important to him that the guys were emotionally okay before they headed home.

The truck also had to be made ready for the next incident. And since his father's job-related cancer, he wanted to make sure the guys followed decontamination protocols on their PPE to remove any potential carcinogens. The silent killer of firefighters.

Like many rural fire companies, the Truelove Fire Department was a combination department that served both commercial and residential properties. There were three full-time employees. Will and his two lieutenants worked forty hours a week. In addition, there were thirteen part-time firefighters like Luke, an administrative assistant and eighteen volunteer firefighters, who were available at a moment's notice.

But whether paid or volunteer, he made sure his crew was trained in a wide variety of fire and rescue specialties, including vehicle extrication and hazardous materials response.

He stuck around to lend a hand, rinsing the hose with dish detergent and water.

"Thanks, Chief." Bradley stowed the last self-contained breathing apparatus on the truck. "We can take it from here."

Will peeled off the latex gloves they used during decontamination and tossed them into the bin.

Nadine waited for him in the doorway of his office. "GeorgeAnne Allen's left half a dozen messages for you, Chief."

He'd been dodging GeorgeAnne's phone calls all week. Relying on ErmaJean to defuse the situation with her fellow matchmaker. Belatedly, he realized he'd never told Kara about the petition. Time to rectify that oversight.

Nadine tilted her head. "Since you missed lunch, maybe you ought to head over to the café and grab a bite to eat."

It was scary sometimes how well Nadine read his mind.

"Good idea." He studied her. "Did you do something different to your hair?" She'd rolled up the back of her hair into some wire device.

"Do you like it?" She touched her updo. "I got to thinking about my mother's French twist roller she wore when I was a little girl. Kara Lockwood's croissant sort of inspired me."

Nadine's new do did kind of remind Will of how the blonde chef wore her hair when she was working. And he totally got how that flaky, delectable pastry could inspire. Kara's croissants were amazing, especially the chocolate ones.

Thoughts of Kara inspired him, too. She was fun. Easy to be with. Gave as good as she got, keeping him on his proverbial toes. And yes, man oh man, could she cook.

Growing up around the firehouse with Pops and a bunch of guys, he'd never really had a female friend before. For a split second, it was like he could hear Bridger's mocking voice in his ear.

Friend? Keep telling yourself that, buddy. Whatever helps you sleep at night.

"Shut up, Bridger Hollingsworth," he muttered and headed toward the open bay. Couldn't a guy just crave a little coffee and dessert?

When Will walked into the café just after two thirty that afternoon, Kara's heart did a happy dance. And it was all she could do to keep the delight off her face.

Especially when, after catching sight of her, his brown eyes gleamed. "Hey, stranger." He sat down on his favorite counter stool.

Yes, he appeared to have claimed a stool for his own.

She bit back a smile. "Hey, yourself." She upturned a

porcelain mug. "Chocolate croissant and a boring cup of American joe?"

The corners of his lips ticked upward. "You know me well."

Ducking her head, she busied herself behind the counter, filling his mug with coffee. He jerked his thumb over his shoulder. "I see Pops is making a nuisance of himself again."

"Your father is a treasure." She flicked her eyes at Will. "And something tells me Mama G doesn't find him a nuisance one bit." Kara slid the plate with the croissant across to him. "I haven't seen her this happy outside her kitchen in years."

The entrance bell jangled. In lavender hospital scrubs, Amber came in with several other women. The pregnant pediatric nurse and her companions waved. Kara waved back. The women settled into one of the booths. Shayla scurried over to take their orders.

He took a sip of coffee. "Making friends, I see."

She smiled. "The moms are on their way to car pool to pick up their children from school. But thanks to Amber, they head over here first to grab a cappuccino and chat."

"I'm glad to hear they're giving you the biz."

"The Mason Jar needs all the happy, loyal patrons it can get." She smoothed her skirt. "I'll just go over and say hello."

She made sure the four women were pleased with their orders and lingered a few moments enjoying feeling part of their friendly group. Amber had been as good as her word introducing her to everyone. The culinary world tended to be dominated by men.

And she relished the opportunity to form some female friendships. Though she was still trying to work through the sometimes tangled, small-town roots of how everyone was connected.

Callie's toddler son batted around an ice cube on the high chair tray. She and Amber had been best friends since high school. The auburn-haired woman smiled at Kara. "We're brainstorming ideas for Lila's wedding to Sam in a few months."

Happiness shone out of ginger-haired Lila's green eyes. Lila was a gifted artist, who ran an arts program at a nearby college. Sam's little girl would also make Lila a new mother as well as a bride. "I love your food, Kara."

"Thank you."

"Do you do any catering?" Lila rested her arms on the tabletop. "We thought we'd found the perfect caterer, but when he found out Truelove was so off the beaten path, he canceled on us."

"That's terrible." She tilted her head. "I haven't really thought about catering, but I suppose I could. Maybe."

An interesting sideline to supplement the Mason Jar's bottom line?

"Oh, that would be great." Lila shifted in the booth toward AnnaBeth. "Perhaps with my wedding director extraordinaire, the three of us could meet tomorrow afternoon when you're less busy to discuss the details."

Flame-haired AnnaBeth whipped out her phone. "That sounds terrific." She consulted her calendar. "What about twoish? I could get my mother-in-law to pick up Hunter from school."

AnnaBeth was married to a handsome cowboy, and their son was a pint-size lasso champion. Kara was slightly in awe of her for several reasons. A social media influencer, AnnaBeth wrote the enormously popular Heart's Home blog. She was an incomer like Kara. And the only one in the group who'd actually been to Paris.

Which was more than Kara had ever managed, but a girl could dream, right?

They were finalizing plans when the front bell jangled again. Maggie, the police chief's wife, swept in with three small preschool boys in tow. One of whom had already stolen Kara's heart.

Seeing her, Maddox rushed forward, grabbing her around her knees. "Miss Karwa!"

Not even trying to hide her smile, she picked him up. "Hey, sweetie pie. Have you had a good day so far?"

Maddox proceeded to give Kara a blow-by-blow description of his ninja warrior class that morning. And a progress report on his latest visit with Soufflé.

She felt rather than saw Will get off the counter stool and come closer. It was like there were extra electrical charges that moved in the air depending on his proximity to her.

AnnaBeth and Lila scooted out from their side of the booth. "Take our seat, Maggie."

The slim, very fit exercise trainer shook her head. "I just came to drop off Maddox with his grandfather." She waved at Pops in the corner booth. "I don't mean to run y'all off."

"Nonsense." AnnaBeth helped Austin scramble into the booth. "Lila and I have to get in line for car pool."

With Will standing beside Kara, goose bumps frolicked like ladybugs across her skin.

"Hey, son."

Maddox gave his dad a brief smile before continuing his monologue to Kara about fishing in the creek that afternoon with Maggie's father and his two best amigos, Austin and Logan.

"Dey have dere own poles and ever-wee-ding, Miss Karwa."

Will rubbed his chin. "I guess dear old dad is nothing but chopped liver when it comes to Miss Kara."

"It's not really me." She fluttered her lashes. "It's my pastry."

He laughed.

Warmth tinged her face. But she'd discovered she adored making him laugh. Most days, due to the cloud hanging over the TFD, he came inside the café looking glum.

The fire chief held out his arms to Maddox. And this time, his son, having ended his tale of today's high adventure, went to his dad.

She'd heard through the Mason Jar customer grapevine that a big town council meeting had happened earlier today. She was guessing it hadn't gone well. His shoulders were broad, but considering the pressure he was under right now, they needed to be broader.

Kara flushed. She shouldn't be thinking of how broad Chief Will MacKenzie's shoulders were or were not.

She did catch Lila exchanging an amused glance with AnnaBeth. "Is it just me or am I wrong in thinking it's a good thing Aunt IdaLee isn't here?"

Was it Kara or had the temperatures inside the café suddenly become like an oven? She fanned her face, grateful Will and Maddox had moved to salivate over the pastry case.

Amber arched her brow. "ErmaJean, too."

Maggie plopped down in the booth. "And especially Aunt GeorgeAnne."

Kara resisted the impulse to grimace. Not a fan of GeorgeAnne Allen. And from what she could gather, the old woman reciprocated her feelings.

But it left a cold, hard knot sitting in the pit of her belly.

Most people liked her. Liked her food, too. She wasn't sure how to handle the older woman's unexpected animosity.

Callie eased the tray off the high chair and unbuckled her son. "I need to get going, too."

Amber inched her way out of the seat. "My belly is growing so big, before long I'm not going to be able to get in the booth at all."

Kara signaled Trudy to take Maggie's order and followed the other moms to the cash register. After they left, she went behind the pastry case.

Using tongs, she removed a chocolate-dipped madeleine from the glass shelf and handed it to Maddox. "A sweet treat for a sweet boy."

Pops ambled over. "Wouldn't mind one of those myself."

Will shook his head, but a smile played about his mouth. "You are spoiling them."

"You want one, too, Chief MacKenzie?" She smirked.

He grinned. "Well, since you're offering…"

Maddox bit into the soft, spongy cookie. "Dank you, Miss Karwa."

Coming around, Kara handed Will a cookie and gave his dear child a hug. Munching his own madeleine, Pops paid his tab. "See you at dinner, son." He departed with Maddox.

Other than Maggie and her boys, the café had emptied out. Only a few more minutes until closing time.

"I don't want to keep you." Still, Will lingered. "I'm sure you have a lot to do."

She could think of nothing she'd rather do than spend all day talking to the fire chief. The prep for tomorrow's specials could wait.

"It's fine." She leaned her hip against the register. "I like talking to you." She went crimson. Had she actually said that out loud?

But a warm light gleamed in his gaze. "I like talking to you, too."

He smiled, causing his eyes to crinkle at the corners. And her knees to wobble. Making her glad she had the counter to lean upon for support.

Will touched the tip of his finger to the silver metal miniature Eiffel Tower she kept beside the register. "Where did this love of all things French come from?"

"From my dad originally." She picked up the mini tower. "We never had much, even when he was alive, although both he and my mom were hard workers. But he always seemed to find enough money for books. The Madeline series was a particular favorite of mine."

She glanced over to where she'd last seen Glorieta, but Mama G had wandered back into the kitchen.

Kara bit her lip. "I don't have a lot of material things from my childhood, but I treasure those books. Mama G has them stored at her house in Durham until I get a permanent address in Truelove."

"May I?" He held out his hand for the metal structure. "I'm not familiar with those children's books."

Placing the miniature into his palm, her mouth quirked. "And why would you be? The Madeline stories tend to be kind of a girl thing."

He examined the silver tower. "I think Maddox's current favorite involves dinosaurs."

"My mother gave me this pint-size version of the Eiffel Tower after my father died in an accident." Kara blew out a breath. "It represented a dream. That better days would come. That one day we'd see Paris."

His gaze caught hers. Her heart dropped to her toes.

"And have you?"

"No, not yet," she whispered.

He handed back the miniature. "One day…" he rasped in his delicious, gravelly voice.

Clutching the tower, she gulped. "One day…"

The bell jangled, and they jolted.

GeorgeAnne stomped inside. "You're a hard man to track down, Chief MacKenzie."

Curiously, his face, normally a healthy tan, paled. "Miss GeorgeAnne."

Determined to be hospitable, Kara plastered a welcoming smile across her features. GeorgeAnne placed the clipboard on top of the pastry case with a flourish.

"What's this?"

GeorgeAnne's mouth thinned. "This is a petition Chief MacKenzie was supposed to present to you earlier this week." She gave Will a starched look. "But seems like it's up to me."

Kara stiffened. "A petition about what?"

Will's Adam's apple bobbed above the open collar of his white uniform shirt. "Kara…"

Maggie got out of the booth. "Aunt GeorgeAnne, what's going on? What have you done?"

Kara looked from her to the old woman. "I'm still not—"

"Signed by over one hundred concerned Truelove citizens." GeorgeAnne tapped her bony finger on the clipboard lying between them. "We demand you put the apple pie back on the menu."

Maggie sucked in a breath. "I'm so sorry. I had no idea."

Kara rounded on Will. "You knew about this?"

He raised his hands. "I—I—"

GeorgeAnne snorted. "His department organized and circulated the petition. The citizens of Truelove are giving you exactly twelve hours to take that apple abomination off the menu and give us back our apple pie, or—"

"Or what?" Crossing her arms, she narrowed her eyes at the old woman.

Perhaps not used to being crossed, GeorgeAnne backed up a step. But a second later she rallied.

"Or... Truelove is going to boycott the Mason Jar." A steely look in her arctic-blue eyes, she jutted her jaw. "And then we'll see how long you stay in business in this town, Miss Lockwood."

Will shook his head. "Can we all discuss this like rational adults?"

She glared at the older woman. "How dare you!" Unfolding, Kara pointed toward the door. "I think you need to leave my restaurant. Now."

With a sniff, GeorgeAnne exited, head held high, nose in the air.

"Kara, if you'd let me explain."

She glowered at him. "I don't think we have anything left to say to each other, *Chief* MacKenzie."

"It's not what it seems."

Kara put the pastry case between them. "Please just go."

Near the booths, Shayla and Trudy stood frozen. Maggie's little boys stared wide-eyed at the loud, adult drama taking place in front of them. Leo poked his torso through the cut-out window to investigate the raised voices.

Glorieta popped her head around the swinging porthole door. "Kara, what's going on?" A puzzled frown creased the barbecue queen's forehead.

The bell jangled, an angry sound. She faced forward again as Will thrust open the door and stalked outside.

With long strides, he headed toward the fire station on the opposite side of the green. Feeling ambushed, she watched him go until tears of anger and betrayal blurred her vision. She swiped at her cheeks.

Her gaze swung toward the witnesses of her utter humiliation. She wished the floor would open up and swallow her.

She realized she was still holding the mini tower in her hand. Gripping it so hard, it would probably leave marks on her palm. Forcing her fingers to relax, she returned the tower to its spot of honor.

Then, shaken and overwhelmed, she sank into a nearby chair.

She hadn't felt this alone since her mother died. *One hundred signatures.* One hundred people hated her food. Hated what she'd done to the Mason Jar. Hated her?

Coming here had been a terrible mistake.

She wished she'd never set eyes on Truelove.

And never met its fire chief.

Chapter Seven

Somehow, Kara managed to hold it together long enough to finish closing the restaurant.

Buying a few colorful macarons for her sons and a caffè mocha to go, Maggie exited amid profuse apologies for her great-aunt's behavior.

Unusually subdued, Trudy retrieved her purse under the counter. Kara was glad when both waitresses and Leo left for the day. Soon, only she and Mama G remained.

"Kara, honey…"

Unable to trust herself to speak, she crossed the dining room. Smoothing her hands down the small white apron she'd worn over her skirt, she pushed through the door into the kitchen. She scrubbed her hands at the sink a little more forcefully than strictly necessary.

This was her favorite time in the café. When for a few hours she had the kitchen all to herself. Switching from acting as hostess to what she really loved—cooking.

Normally, she tallied receipts, tracked inventory and placed orders for additional supplies. She'd evaluate the success of today's dishes. What had gone right. What had gone wrong. What she had missed. What missing ingredient could have made the difference.

Had its execution been on point? How might she have improved its taste and flavor for patrons?

Or had it lain on the plate, flat and uninspiring to her diners? Kind of how she felt right now about the Mason Jar.

What had she done wrong? What had she missed? What else could she have done to make the citizens of Truelove love her food versus hating it?

She slipped into her chef whites and took out the ingredients for tomorrow's baked goods. Flour. Butter. Cream. Eggs. At the prep counter, she felt a whoosh of air behind her. She should've known Mama G wouldn't let this go.

"We need to talk about what happened with GeorgeAnne Allen, sugar."

Her back still turned, she closed her eyes. "If you don't mind, I'd rather not. Not right now. I've got a ton of—"

"What I mind is you stuffing your emotions down like you'd stuff a Christmas goose. You've got every right to feel angry. I'm angry, too."

Kara's eyes flew open and she turned on her heel. "My galette is a signature dish. It's won awards."

Mama G folded her arms over her massive bosom. "That old woman had no right to come into your establishment with her demands." She wagged her finger. "Much less threaten your livelihood."

"Exactly." Kara widened her stance. "How dare she?"

"How dare she indeed." Mama G bobbed her head. "But keeping it bottled up inside isn't healthy. Don't let the anger marinate. That only leads to bitterness." Her foster mom arched her eyebrow. "And bitterness isn't a flavor a chef of your caliber should cultivate."

As usual, Mama G was right.

"I think the bigger question is, what do you plan to do about the petition? What will be your response?"

Kara planted her hands on her hips. "A chef has the right to set the menu, especially in her own restaurant."

"That is entirely true." Glorieta pursed her lips. "And customers also have the right not to eat it."

"So the customer is always right?" Kara gaped at her. "You think I should just give in? Drop the apple galette and reinstate the pie?"

"That's not what I'm saying." Glorieta held Kara's gaze. "Sometimes the customer doesn't understand what would truly please them. They may not know until you've shown it to them first. But it doesn't hurt to examine the situation from GeorgeAnne's point of view."

"Did you look at the names on the petition?" Kara threw up her hands. "Some of those people I believed to be new friends. And to think that Will MacKenzie—"

"Yes, do let's discuss the young fire chief."

But that was the last thing she wanted to do. Gritting her teeth, she got out a glass mixing bowl from the shelf below.

Glorieta leaned against the stainless-steel counter. "I know that you're hurt, but I think you should let him explain. He seemed as upset about the petition as you were."

Baring her teeth, Kara one-handed an egg and cracked it with a two-fingered, expert trick she'd learned from Mama G, not from culinary school. "I can promise you he's not as upset as me."

The yolky contents fell into the bowl. Perfect every time. She tossed the crumpled, empty shell aside.

Kara cracked another egg. "What would you do in this situation?"

"It doesn't matter what I'd do." Glorieta took off her hat. "I don't think that is for me to say."

"So now you decide to go all 'silent partner' on me?" Kara huffed. She reached for another egg.

"I will say I think you need to seek the Lord's counsel in how to proceed."

Kara's hand convulsed around the egg, crushing it. Egg whites, yolk and shell fell into the bowl. She groaned.

"Don't give in to despair. All is not lost." Glorieta handed her a clean dish towel. "You can't make an omelet without breaking a few eggs first. Hang in there, sugar."

Mama G headed back to the motel. Kara was grateful to be left alone to blow off some steam and ponder her next move.

That night Will tried to call her. She guessed he'd begged her number off ErmaJean. Confined to his crate, Soufflé meowed.

But each time her cell rang, she promptly hit Ignore. And she lay awake half the night fretting over what Friday morning would bring.

She need not have worried. A steady stream of customers cycled in and out. And that afternoon an especially large crowd filled every seat as the apple pie deadline drew closer.

Kara was feeling mildly triumphant, like she'd dodged a bullet. Like GeorgeAnne didn't wield the social clout she thought she did. Then Trudy burst her bubble.

"Folks are here for the biggest show in town." At the pass-through window, the bottle-blonde waitress dinged the bell for service. "Order up!" she bellowed.

Plating orders in the kitchen, Glorieta clattered a pan. Leo rattled a skillet on the grill. The vent above the stovetop hummed.

Kara blinked. "What show?"

"The showdown." Trudy moved to the ice dispenser. "No one wanted to miss your reaction to the ultimatum."

Last night she'd decided to ignore the deadline. To keep

calm and carry on. The apple tart galette would remain on the menu.

The deadline came and went. The restaurant emptied of customers. GeorgeAnne had the good sense not to show her face. For which Kara was grateful.

But Fire Chief MacKenzie didn't make an appearance, either. And she couldn't decide if she was relieved by his absence, or if that only made her madder at him.

It quickly became clear who were Kara's true friends. Late Friday afternoon she wondered if AnnaBeth and Lila might prove a no-show for the catering consultation, but they arrived right on time, eager to talk wedding food.

Kara led them to an empty booth. Plenty to choose from. If this afternoon was any indication of things to come, catering might become crucial to keeping the lights on and her staff employed.

"Sam and I don't want anything extravagant."

Lila probably didn't even realize how her voice changed when she said her fiancé's name. Kara had met Sam last week. He owned a commercial and residential paint contracting business.

AnnaBeth nodded. "It's going to be held at the Field-Stone for family and close friends."

Her cowboy husband, Jonas, operated the successful dude ranch. Kara hadn't been out there yet, but the facilities and the views were reputed to be stellar.

They discussed menu options, and she scrolled through the photos she'd brought up on her cell to show them. For a pleasant hour, they chatted, making decisions. She was able to temporarily step outside the turmoil and dwell on happier things.

"What about the wedding cake?" Lila pulled a picture out of her purse. "I saw this in a magazine."

"Despite the pastry case, baking really isn't my forte."

She'd gone through the required courses at culinary school, but had chosen to concentrate on cooking, not baking. The elaborate icing scrollwork in the photo was definitely outside her skill set.

Kara chewed her lip. "But I have a friend who works in a bakery in Asheville who does cakes on the side. Which, by the way, are amazing. How about I give you her number?"

Lila smiled. "That sounds wonderful. Thank you. For everything."

That night Will texted her. But she deleted the messages without reading them. Mama G and Pops had gone to a movie over at the county seat. To offset the thundering quiet in her house, she talked to the cat while preparing a light meal. Soufflé had proven to be good company.

"Better than several humans I know," she muttered, stroking a finger along the tabby's cream-colored fur.

And then Saturday morning arrived.

It was obvious from the outset that the usual weekend crowd was down. No line. No waiting. Too many unoccupied tables.

"Miss Kara." Shayla stopped on her way to deliver a carafe of coffee to the usual Saturday Breakfast Date couples—Myra Penry, Wilda Arledge and Deirdre Fleming, who'd arrived without their husbands this morning. "Have you looked out the window lately?"

She swung around. Outside on the sidewalk across the street, GeorgeAnne waved a poster board on a stick.

It read in large black letters—We Want Apple Pie.

She clamped her jaw shut to keep it from quivering, but the bottom dropped out of her stomach.

"GeorgeAnne better have a permit," Wilda, Police Chief Hollingsworth's mom, growled. "I'm calling Bridger."

Kara could've cried when Reverend Bryant walked boldly past GeorgeAnne's gauntlet and entered the Mason Jar.

She clutched a menu to her chest. "Thank you for coming today, Pastor."

He gave her a kind smile. "Not going to miss my mocha fix. And I thought you could use the support. GeorgeAnne doesn't speak for everyone in this community."

But it became obvious very quickly who was Team Kara and who...was not.

At lunch ErmaJean and IdaLee arrived. On the sidewalk, heated words were exchanged with their fellow Double Name Club member. Their voices carried through the plate-glass windows. Kara winced.

"I hope you do not think, GeorgeAnne Allen, that you can tell me what to do." Head held high, IdaLee marched inside.

"Right is right." Sniffing, ErmaJean made to follow IdaLee. "And wrong is wrong, GeorgeAnne."

Tray tucked under her arm, Trudy shook her head. "I never thought I'd live to see the matchmakers squabbling among themselves."

People were taking sides. Which only served to make her feel even lower. To have brought such division to harmonious Truelove. It made her physically sick to her stomach.

Sunday morning she debated whether or not to attend church with Glorieta. She had no desire to bring conflict into the house of God.

"You've done nothing wrong." Glorieta adjusted her hat in the hall mirror at Kara's rented house. The barbecue queen couldn't abide people not looking their best on the Lord's Day. "The pie versus galette situation is simply a matter of a difference of opinion. It's GeorgeAnne Allen who's escalated this. I can think of at least twelve ways to Sunday this could've been handled better."

"For sure."

Her foster mom cut her eyes at Kara. "On both sides."

Kara frowned.

"But I'm prayed up on the 'love your enemies' part," Glorieta said while settling her voluminous yellow purse on her arm. "So I figure my heart is ready to go to Sunday meeting and fellowship with my Lord."

Prayer and loving her enemy—neither of which Kara had yet brought herself to do.

She finally decided to go with Glorieta. If she chose to stay home, it would be a slap in the face to Reverend Bryant, who'd braved the wrath of GeorgeAnne on her behalf.

And also because she refused to let GeorgeAnne win.

Okay, not the best attitude. She was still reeling. Her attitude was a work in progress.

Glorieta headed out to the car. "But GeorgeAnne Allen better not come at my girl," her foster mother harrumphed. "'Cause I'm not that prayed up. Not yet."

Kara bit off a smile. Her fears regarding church proved groundless. It was GeorgeAnne who didn't attend. And of course, Will MacKenzie wasn't a churchgoer, either. So no danger of running into him there.

One more example of how they would never suit each other. Reverend Bryant chose as his selected passage that morning, "Blessed are the peacemakers. For they shall be called the children of God."

Glorieta elbowed her. Kara fidgeted.

However, as the last hymn washed over her, the remembered pain in Will's voice when he talked about his past made her wish—no matter her own feelings about him at the moment—he could find the kind of peace that only came from God.

The next day Monday's patronage was worse than the weekend. GeorgeAnne was back out there on the sidewalk with her sign, too. And one of the volunteer firefighters joined her. A gangly limbed young man, Kara recognized as Lila Penry's cousin, Zach.

His sign said Pie or Die.

Which seemed overstated, if not also melodramatic. At least, from her point of view.

She pinched the bridge of her nose. She couldn't bear the idea of laying off her employees. *Why is this happening, Lord?*

Over the next few, long, excruciating days, she made several observations. Based on her current clientele, the majority of the female population of Truelove appreciated the culinary additions she'd added to the Mason Jar menu. But the men—*thank you very much, you traitorous fire chief*—did not.

Including the entire daily breakfast club of ROMEOs—Retired Older Men Eating Out. With the exception of Pops.

Every day as soon as he dropped Maddox off at preschool, Will's father arrived to claim his favorite seat, his favorite café au lait, settling in for his daily chat with Glorieta. And on Wednesday after the café closed, dear, loyal Pops brought in Maddox for a previously arranged cooking lesson.

Seeing the little boy and enjoying his exuberant hugs did much to restore her faith in humanity and her self-esteem as anything else. Spending time with him in the kitchen was a joy. She thoroughly enjoyed icing the cupcakes they baked. And from the buttercream icing he somehow managed to smear all over his face, she believed he did, too.

Glorieta delayed her return home to Durham. Adding to Kara's guilt. "Only until the trouble blows over, sugar pie."

Which, as the boycott continued, Kara despaired of

ever actually happening. Since his abortive text messages over the weekend, she hadn't heard anything from Will. Apparently, the fire chief had moved on from their failed-to-thrive friendship.

If that is indeed what she'd felt for him. Past tense. At least she'd discovered his true measure before she'd fallen in love with him.

Oh really? Sure about that, are you?

That evening, mindful of the splint, she cradled Soufflé in her lap. "Good riddance to him."

Now, if only she could make her heart believe it.

Later, lonely and filled with nervous energy, she was getting ready to roll out a ball of dough when there was a knock at the back door.

Soufflé meowed from his crate on the stool.

Wiping her hands on her cherry blossom apron, Kara twitched aside the lace panel curtain. Her pulse zinged at the sight of the handsome fire chief standing on the stoop.

"Please, Kara," he said through the glass pane separating them. "I can't stand this distance between us."

She put her hand to her throat in a vain attempt to slow her breathing and the too-rapid beating of her heart that just seeing him always wrought.

He stuffed his hands in his pockets and peered at her through the glass. "Please. Can we talk?"

Today had been the continuation of the town council's discussion on the future of the TFD. He looked weary and utterly spent. And so alone.

The yearning in his voice matched the yearning in her heart, and before she could talk herself out of it, she flung open the door.

When she thrust open the door so forcefully, Will wasn't sure if he should step inside or beat a hasty retreat.

Not able to talk to her, he'd endured a miserable week. Knowing she felt hurt and betrayed by him. Akin to what he'd felt when Liz walked away.

Only this time, he was the one who'd inflicted the pain. And he was ashamed of himself. For not putting a stop to GeorgeAnne's schemes when he had the chance.

"Hi." He flushed. *So lame.* He tried again. "I've come to ask you to forgive me."

She frowned. "How did the council meeting go today?"

He shook his head. "Not good. They postponed the vote for further review." But if she was concerned about his TFD meeting with the council members, maybe she didn't totally hate his guts, after all.

Throughout the week he'd listened hungrily to every morsel of information Maddox and Pops shared about their time with Kara. It was beyond humiliating to admit he was jealous of his three-year-old son and sixty-five-year-old father, but he was.

It surprised him how much he missed seeing her every day. Laughing with her. Teasing her. And the verbal volleys she never failed to lob his way in response.

"Since you're here—" she stepped away from the door "—I guess you might as well come inside."

Not the most welcoming invitation he'd ever received, but he'd take what he could get.

Soufflé meowed in what he interpreted as a greeting. Crate door open, like a king in his palace, the tabby lay stretched on his side with his gimpy leg in a splint.

"Oh." He stared at the blob of dough on the floured countertop. "I've interrupted you."

She put the counter between them. "I can talk and roll out this dough at the same time." She smacked her fist in the middle of the ball, squashing the dough flat.

He swallowed, wondering if that was his head she was

imagining. "I should've done more to head GeorgeAnne off at the pass. I guess I was hoping it would blow over. I had no idea she would show up at the Mason Jar like that."

She didn't say anything. He spent the next few moments watching her roll the dough into a ball and punch it down again. Each time, he winced.

He inserted a finger inside his collar.

Brandishing a rolling pin, she cut her eyes at him. "Was the petition your idea?"

"No. But I allowed myself for the sake of the department to be pressured into being the front man. At the time, I didn't realize you were the target."

She stilled.

He caught her gaze. "I would never have agreed if I'd realized you were the owner of the Mason Jar."

She swiped her cheek with the back of her hand, leaving a streak of flour.

He pointed.

"What?"

"Your face."

She scowled at him. "What's wrong with my face?"

"Absolutely nothing, but you've got flour on your cheek." He gulped. "And I'm doing everything in my power to resist touching your beautiful face." He eyed the rolling pin in her hands. "Since the first day we met, I've found you completely irresistible, but right now I fear bodily harm."

Her mouth twitched.

"Be brave, Will MacKenzie." She laid her hands flat on the wooden counter. "I dare you to get the flour off my face. And I promise I won't brain you." She cocked her head. "Wouldn't want to damage my expensive rolling pin on your hard noggin."

Her eyes locked on to his. And this time he saw the invitation he'd waited for. Reaching across the counter, he brushed the flour off the apple of her cheek with the pad of his thumb.

At the touch of his fingers against her skin, she inhaled sharply. But she didn't drop her gaze. His heart drummed inside his chest.

He cupped her face in the palm of his hand. "I missed you, Kara," he rasped.

She took a quick, deep, shuddering breath. The way Maddox did after he'd been crying too hard for too long. "I missed you, too," she whispered.

A small—growing ever smaller—part of him worried a little at how fundamentally necessary Kara Lockwood had become to his world. But he reasoned it was entirely understandable. It had been three years since he'd looked at a woman. Much less found her companionable and attractive.

It was okay to admit he was attracted to her. That he liked her, which sounded so high school. But *like* was as far as he was prepared to go. Could go. And as long as he planted his feet firmly on this side of like, he ought to be fine. Everything under control.

He tucked back a lock of hair that had come loose from the bun on the back of her head. His hand, seemingly possessing a will of its own, lingered. He stared into her eyes. "Can you forgive me for not being the sort of man you deserve?"

"I forgive you." She tilted her head. "What do you want from me, Will?"

Everything. But he didn't say that. Once erected, barricades weren't so easily deconstructed.

"I'd like to spend more time with you, Kara."

She looked at him. "I'd like that, too. Have you eaten dinner?"

He leaned on the counter. "You don't have to feed me every time I see you."

She scraped the dough off the wooden butcher block and threw it into a bin. "Overworked," she said to his raised eyebrow. "And I like feeding you. So let me."

His mouth curved. "I can do that."

"Good." She drew out a skillet from a bottom cabinet. "Nothing fancy. How about crêpes?" She threw him a mischievous grin over her shoulder.

"Can I help?"

She looked up at him. "I'd like that. More than I can say."

Him, too.

She pulled a container out of the fridge. "I mixed up the batter earlier. It's been chilling for about an hour. But I'd lost my appetite until just now." She buttered the skillet and turned on the gas burner.

Kara poured a small amount of batter into the pan and did a twirling motion, stretching the batter to the edges of the skillet.

"So it's like a really thin pancake?"

"Watch this." She winked. "You might want to back up a step." Gripping the handle, she gave the skillet a huge circular shake and flipped the crêpe. "Voilà!"

He grinned. "Now you're just showing off."

"The higher you flip it, the longer the time you have to catch it." She laughed. "It's all in the wrist."

Using up the rest of the batter, she made a nice stack of the delicate-as-lace crêpes. "Now we add filling. This is where you can help me. You can be my sous-chef."

Working alongside her, he added bits of tomato, bacon, chopped ham and sprigs of parsley. Their shoulders touched, and occasionally his hand brushed hers. Which was okay.

More than okay.

They sat across from each other in the small breakfast nook. She'd managed to make even her version of a simple meal an elegant affair. While they ate, they chatted about favorite things.

He glanced around the cozy kitchen. She was renting the house from Bridger's mom. But somehow Kara's little touches made it look like a real home. "How is Soufflé?"

Scraping back her chair, she took his plate over to the sink. "The tabby had a follow-up with the veterinarian this week. Dr. Abernathy thinks the splint can come off soon."

Plugging the sink, she squirted dishwashing detergent into the basin and turned on the faucet.

"Here. Let me do that." He rose from the table. "Mac-Kenzie family rules. You cook. I clean."

She moved aside to allow him access to the sink. "For dessert, I can use the rest of the crêpes to make a sweet treat."

His forearms sudsy, he shook his head. "Do you ever stay still for one moment?" He rinsed a plate. "You're treat enough. But I'll take a rain—"

"Rain check." Taking it from him, she dried the plate with a cloth. "The kitchen is my happy place."

"What drew you to cooking?"

She opened the oak cabinet and stretching on her toes, she put away the plate. "After the chaos of my childhood, I found it orderly. Soothing. Comforting."

He handed her another plate to dry. He hoped one day she'd trust him enough to tell him of the time before Glorieta Ferguson came into her life.

Kara swiped the lingering moisture from the rooster-red plate. "Recipes are instructions. And if you followed the directions—"

"Voilà!" He smiled.

She flicked her eyes at him. His heart skipped a beat. She absolutely could not know how cute she looked, or the effect she had on his equilibrium.

"Voilà—everything turns out wonderful." She put the plate on top of the other inside the cabinet. "I feel in control when I cook. And safe."

"It's a shame life doesn't come with instructions like a recipe," he grunted.

Her forehead puckered. Something she did when she was concentrating. He resisted the urge to smooth the line from her brow.

"I think life is best lived when we give control over to God." She bit her lip. "That's probably the biggest thing Mama G taught me. God promises to make everything work out exactly as it should. When I trust Him, there's no safer place to be." She shook herself. "Sorry to get so… philosophical."

He grabbed her hand. "I want to know what you're thinking and feeling. I've felt so distant from God."

"I think God is closer than you believe, Will." She twined her fingers in his, suds and all. "I struggle, too. Especially lately."

"What're you going to do about the boycott?"

She let go of him. "I've been thinking about it. Nonstop. Except when I was thinking of you." She gave him that look again.

And he nearly dropped the glass. "Are you flirting with me, Chef Lockwood?"

She smirked. "Possibly, Chief MacKenzie."

"I've thought about you, too." He handed the glass into her custody. "So are you replacing the galette with the pie?"

"Uh, no." Her mouth downturned. "But I've decided to

fight GeorgeAnne's bad press about the Mason Jar with good press. And woo Truelove back to the café."

He leaned his elbows on the rim of the porcelain sink. "Kill 'em with kindness."

"I wish I could make things better for you and the TFD."

He glanced at the crêpe skillet, waiting to be washed. "You know, I might just have an idea of how you can do both. In a couple of weeks, the TFD will hold its annual pancake supper fund-raiser."

She narrowed her eyes. "Pancake supper?"

"The Truelove Firefighter Auxiliary sponsors the event on the first Saturday in April to raise money for the Firefighter Cancer Fund." He straightened. "Like with Pops, cancer has become an occupational hazard for firefighters."

"One of my greatest desires was to become part of Truelove's community." She put away the glass. "I'd be happy to donate supplies and cook, too. Serve in any capacity you need me."

He shook his head. "The auxiliary organizes everything. They set up tables and chairs on the green. Buy supplies. Sell tickets. The crew cooks the pancakes. Everyone in Truelove comes out for it." He rinsed off a bundle of silverware. "But what would you think of a Flapjack Flip-Off this year?"

"A what?"

"My guys cook the pancakes, but you and your crew make…" He brandished the skillet.

"Crêpes aren't flapjacks, Will. Nor pancakes, either."

He waved his hand, spattering a few drops of water on the countertop. "Sounds more alliterative, though." He grinned, warming to his idea. "It's all you can eat. Truelove citizens vote for their favorite—pancakes or crêpes. A cooking contest and a fund-raiser."

"But a competition?" She made a face. "I don't know. I'd lose without a doubt."

He unplugged the sink. "I wouldn't be so sure of that." Water gurgled out. "Wasn't it you who told me the owner has confidence in her food?"

"It would certainly allow the public to form their own opinions about my food and not be held hostage by GeorgeAnne's apple pie bias." She slumped. "On the other hand, if it goes badly, it could be the nail in the Mason Jar's coffin."

"Not going to happen. I've eaten your crêpes." He took both of her hands enfolded by the dish towel into his. "And trust me, darlin', there's no way you'll lose."

He found his mouth very close to hers. If he moved his head... Did she want to kiss him as badly as he wanted to kiss her?

She smelled amazing. Like vanilla. He leaned forward. Her lips parted. His heart stopped. Her lashes fluttered.

But then...he pulled back. "Tomorrow night. My house. We can go over Flapjack Flip-Off details."

She slid her hands away from his, leaving him standing there holding the dishcloth. "Only if you let me cook."

"As if Maddox would have it any other way." He took a deep breath. "I promise you won't regret taking this chance."

"I won't, because only with great risk—" rising on the toes of her ballet-type flats, she gave him a quick kiss on his cheek "—comes great reward." Coming down on her heels, she smiled at him.

And he resolved to do whatever he must to make this work for her.

If he gazed long enough in the liquid blue pools of her eyes, he believed he might drown. But for once, he didn't care.

Chapter Eight

Friday proved an abysmally slow day for the café.

Kara had never been good with too much time on her hands. Thankfully as a distraction, AnnaBeth showed up for lunch. And with the sparse crowd, Kara had time to join her.

Giving her the grand tour, she took AnnaBeth through to the kitchen into the heart of the operation.

"We prep and plate over here." She pointed. "And place the orders at the cut-out window behind the counter for pickup into the dining room."

She swung open the heavy, insulated door of the walk-in freezer. Both women shivered at the blast of refrigerated air.

A pair of suspended air conditioners lowered the ceiling about two feet. Bulky steel shelving with boxed cases of inventory took up most of the freezer space and left only a few feet of standing room between the shelves.

She and AnnaBeth ended up eating in her tiny office, which consisted of a chair, a chair for guests and a desk overflowing with paperwork.

Kara showed AnnaBeth the cooking journals on the shelf behind her desk. Over the years she'd recorded every recipe she ever tried. Some were disasters. Others were triumphs.

But she also jotted down her thoughts over each ingredient. Every step in the process. Her ideas and tweaks.

The journals represented her culinary journey thus far. An irreplaceable map of where she'd been and how far she'd come.

AnnaBeth shared her struggles with self-worth. And the wisdom she'd learned about her identity in Christ. Kara could hardly believe how much the glamorous fashionista had doubted herself.

She told AnnaBeth about her lifelong dream of one day visiting Paris. And since the style blogger was interested in interior design, Kara found the courage to take another album off the shelf, containing paint swatches and photos of her ideas for transforming the Mason Jar into an authentic Paris bistro.

"I only had enough money to give the Mason Jar a facelift, not a complete overhaul. But one day…"

AnnaBeth's eyes gleamed. "I love imagining the possibilities of *one day*."

"I didn't want to ruffle community feathers in Truelove so I saved most of my changes for the menu." Kara grimaced. "And we see how well that's going."

AnnaBeth looked at the time on her cell. "This has been so fun, but I promised to tutor a child at Hunter's school this afternoon." She rose.

Kara came around her desk. "Let's do this again."

"Soon." AnnaBeth settled her purse strap on her shoulder. "I've been brainstorming ways to increase the café's revenue and raise your profile. But I'm not sure you'll be interested."

Kara threw open her hands. "Are you kidding me? I'm game for anything if it will pay the bills."

"What would you think about being a weekly guest video blogger?" AnnaBeth panned the air with her hands. "Classy But Easy French Cooking tutorials."

Kara's mouth dropped. "Me? On video?"

AnnaBeth's blog had a national following.

"You'd be a natural." She smiled. "It could drive a lot of tourist traffic off the Blue Ridge Parkway to your restaurant, too. Maybe even attract people from as far away as Asheville, Charlotte or Winston-Salem. A win for you, and a win for Truelove."

"I don't know what to say."

AnnaBeth squeezed her arm. "Say yes. You won't have to do this alone. I promise to help."

Kara took a deep breath. "Okay, then. Yes." She shook her head, amazed. "And thanks."

On the threshold, AnnaBeth did an elegant turn on her heels. "What else are friends for? I'm just so sorry Miss GeorgeAnne's antics have tarnished your view of our little mountain town. It's the most wonderful place in the world." She winked. "Where true love awaits."

Kara crossed her arms. "I'm going to plead the fifth on that one."

"Don't be too sure, my friend. I was running away from love, too." An amused smile crossed AnnaBeth's striking features. "Right up until I ran into a certain cowboy in Truelove. And it hasn't escaped anyone's notice how you light up when a particular fire chief comes into the café."

Kara blushed. "Is it that obvious?"

"As obvious as when Will MacKenzie looks back at you."

Kara sucked in a breath. "He looks at me?"

She laughed. "No doubt about it." With a flutter of her fingers, AnnaBeth departed.

About six that evening Kara pulled into Will's driveway.

Pops had insisted on going to the market for the items on tonight's menu. Will's dad dropped them off to her at the Jar. Then declared he was joining Tom and Wilda Arledge for dinner at their farmhouse. Kara also had it on good authority that Glorieta would be accompanying them.

For a moment she remained in the car, studying the MacKenzie house. She had a thing about houses. The two-story brick house with the Dutch gambrel roof looked like a real home.

It was where Will had grown up. Vacant for a few years when his parents temporarily relocated to be closer to him and Maddox in Charlotte.

But after the death of his mother, Will had taken the TFD fire chief position and returned. Grabbing her canvas shopping totes, she got out of the car. Her heart melted when she saw Maddox on the other side of the storm door. Waiting for her. And behind him, Will.

Her heart did a staccato step. What would it be like to call this house her home? What would it be like to come home after a long day at the café to a family? *Her* family.

The fire chief threw open the door, and Maddox flung his arms around her.

Will raised his eyebrows. "Somebody's glad to see you."

She cocked her hip. "Is he the only one?"

"No." Will looked at her. "He's not."

Smiling to beat the band, she stepped inside.

Will took the shopping bags out of her hands. "This way to the kitchen. Excuse the mess. Remember, this is the domain of bachelors."

It wasn't a mess. She followed him toward the back. The house could benefit, however, from a woman's touch.

Maddox hopped up on a stool. Will unloaded the groceries. She preheated the oven.

"What culinary delight are you making tonight?"

She pulled out a shallow baking pan. "Salmon en papillote. And before you ask, that means salmon wrapped in parchment paper."

He grinned.

"It will take about thirty minutes, but I made something else for swectie pie I thought he would enjoy more. A ham and cheese croissant."

"Good call." He lifted Maddox off the stool. "Let's set the table for Kara, buddy."

She placed fresh asparagus and thin strips of carrot on the heart-shaped piece she'd cut from parchment paper. She topped the vegetables with the salmon filet.

While crimping the parchment edges to facilitate steaming the salmon, she watched Will and Maddox through the doorway into the dining room. For a split second, she let herself dream that Will was her husband. That Maddox called her Mommy.

That there was a small herb garden beyond the screened porch in the backyard. That this house was her home. This kitchen, hers to decorate in classic, French-inspired hues of buttery yellow, paprika red and country blue. A beautiful place of warmth, good food, love and laughter.

In the dining room Maddox said something silly. Will picked him up, slung his giggling son over his shoulders and hauled him firefighter-style into the kitchen.

Later, Maddox wanted Kara to read to him. Will insisted on cleaning the kitchen, although she protested.

"MacKenzie rules. You cook. I clean."

"All right. If you insist."

Maddox had on his red-and-black fire truck pajamas. They cuddled together against the pillows on his bed. He'd chosen three books. One was about a talking yellow backhoe. The second involved blue trains. Will slipped into his son's room as she picked up the last one.

"One of my favorites," she said, looking at the cover. *"Blueberries for Sal."*

Maddox snuggled under her arm. "I wuv bwoo-beweez, Miss Karwa."

She kissed the top of his head. "Me, too." He smelled of baby shampoo and...a trace of his dad's cologne. In other words, just right.

The book was about the joy of an ordinary day. Every day she spent with Maddox and his father felt extraordinary and filled to the brim with joy. Perhaps this summer they could go berry picking on the mountain. Minus the bear.

When she finished, Will asked her to stay to tuck in Maddox for the night. Tears sprang to her eyes as he helped Maddox say his prayers.

Despite his own struggles, Will was trying to encourage his son's faith. And it reinforced what she already knew about the fire chief. He was a good man. An incredible man. So worth knowing.

Afterward, they said good-night to the yawning child. Will flipped the light switch, and they tiptoed out to the living room. "That meant the world to Maddox."

"You are a great dad."

He gave her a smile that lifted his entire face, laugh lines fanning out from his dark eyes. "Thank you, Kara. As a single parent, it's so easy to focus on what I can't give him, instead of all that I do."

Sitting down on the couch, she reached into her purse and got out her notebook. "We should talk about the Flip-Off."

He lowered himself at the other end of the sofa. It didn't take long to hammer out the details. During which the distance between them on the couch mysteriously lessened. Not that she minded.

She settled into the cushion. "What was it like growing up in Truelove?"

"For an outdoorsy guy like me, it was fabulous." He gestured. "The mountains. The river. But back then, I couldn't wait to get away." He leaned forward and propped his elbows on his knees. "Kind of ironic when you consider I'd do anything now to never have to leave again."

"I'm praying you won't have to." She tilted her head. "You've mentioned Maddox's health issues when he was born. Is he okay now?"

"Right as rain." Will smiled. "Thanks for asking. He had some developmental delays that required therapy for a time, but he's completely caught up with his age group and doing great."

"He's a sweetheart."

Will nudged her with his shoulder. "Takes after his dad."

She rolled her eyes. "He takes after his grandfather."

They smiled at each other.

"I feel like you know everything about me." Will sat back. "But I know very little about your life."

She looked away. "I told you about the time I came to Truelove as a child. About my dad. My mom. Culinary school."

"Glorieta came into your life after your mom died. That must have been so hard. To lose your mom and then to go live with a stranger."

Her eyes flitted to him. "Glorieta wasn't a stranger."

"I see."

But she could tell from the question in his gaze that he really didn't. Her heart stutter-stepped. Torn between full disclosure and self-protection. The retelling brought up painful memories.

He'd shared so much of his difficulties with her. About

his failed marriage. His son's medical crisis. How could she not be as open as he'd been with her?

She hugged the couch pillow to her chest. Creating space. But was that what she really wanted? Space between her and Will?

Kara sighed. "After my father was killed in the construction accident, there was a problem with the insurance."

"You don't have to—"

"I want to tell you." She swallowed. "It—it's just hard. I'm afraid you'll think less of me. See me differently."

He took hold of her hand. "I could never think less of you. And I already know what I need to know about you. That you're kind, generous and good."

Taking courage from his words, she took a deep breath. "My mother got sick. Unable to work consistently, she couldn't pay the rent. We were evicted from our apartment in Durham." Kara slipped her hand from his. "So from the age of eight until I was about ten, we lived out of her car."

He sucked in a breath. "I'm so sorry, Kara."

She dropped her gaze. "The streets were scary at night." She shuddered. "We had no place to go. No one to turn to. I watched my mom choose to not eat so the little money she scraped together could feed me. But even with her sacrifice, I remember always being hungry."

"And you've made it your life mission to feed people."

She looked up. "People wonder how what happened to us could happen in America. The land of plenty. Yet, we fell through the cracks, and no one noticed."

His brow furrowed. "But your teachers…"

"It's hard to pay attention when your stomach hurts. I fell asleep a lot in class. The other children…" She bit her lip.

Even now, the memory brought incredible shame. As

an adult, she understood the shame wasn't deserved, but every time she thought of those terrible times, the shame rushed in all the same, like a flood.

"They called me names," she whispered. "Because my clothes were dirty. And I smelled." She kneaded the cushion between her hands. "It became easier not to go to school." Tears stung her eyes, blurring her vision. "No one missed me. I used to pass the other kids' nice houses and wish I lived there. The ones with the pretty yards. And I'd imagine what life would be like if I were them."

"Kara." He tipped up her chin with his forefinger. "Look at me, darlin'."

Salty tears ran down her cheeks. "My mother did the best she could, but she was so sick. Perhaps if she'd had access to proper medical care in the beginning, she wouldn't have died." She gave a small, helpless shrug. "That's one of the hardest parts. The never knowing."

He opened his arms. And without a second's hesitation, she went into them. Tucked under his chin, he stroked her hair and she closed her eyes. He made her feel so safe. So protected.

And loved? She was almost too afraid to hope for that. Her childhood had taught her to not expect too much.

"There were shelters for people like uh—us," her voice quavered.

Will's arms tightened around her.

"Homeless people like me. Except, there were never enough beds. But when I was about ten, we got a spot that particular night. Mom was so tired. By that point, she slept a lot."

She brushed her cheek against the denim of his shirt. He smelled so good. Like outdoors. A spicy cologne. And something that was just him. Manly.

"It wasn't suppertime yet, but my stomach ached. I

could smell the food being prepared in the shelter's kitchen. So I crept downstairs to where the volunteers were preparing dinner. I hid in the pantry. From the aromas, I tried to identify what was for supper. The tomatoey smell of the Brunswick stew simmering on the stovetop. The tangy vinegar scent of barbecue pork."

He raised his head. "Glorieta."

"Area restaurants took turns volunteering at the soup kitchen. Mama G found me huddled in the pantry." Kara squeezed her eyes shut. "She had on this funny hat with a bold pattern of yellows, reds and greens. She gave me a corn stick to munch on, wrapped a small towel around my waist and put me to work stirring green beans in a pot."

Her ear pressed against his chest, she took reassurance from the steady beat of his heart.

"Glorieta saved me. I owe her everything. She found a long-term family shelter for us and arranged palliative care for my mother at the last stage of her life. At my mother's funeral, which Mama G paid for, she asked me if I'd like to go live with her and the boys. And the rest, as they say, is history."

She held her breath, relishing the comfort of his arms. *Just one minute more, please, Lord.* Before he thrust her away. She dreaded the moment she had to look into his eyes. To see herself in his gaze as a less-than. The disgust. The judgment. Like so many did when they learned of her background.

"You are the bravest person I've ever known."

"That's not true." She sat up. "You're a firefighter. You show real bravery every day."

He caught her face in his hands. His strong, warm hands. His calloused, yet gentle, palms against her cheeks. "Real courage is more than running into a fire. Real courage is hanging in there, through thick and thin instead of running away." He brushed his lips against her forehead. "And when I look at you, I see the most beautiful, most courageous woman I've ever known."

He stroked her cheeks with his thumbs. "Your triumph over that background only makes me long to know you even more."

Relief that he understood—that he got her—left her feeling suddenly weak. And spent.

"Maddox isn't the only one who loves blueberries."

Her mouth curved. "Oh?"

"Yep." He grinned. "And every time I look into your eyes, I'm reminded how much I really love blueberries."

She batted her lashes at him. "Is that so?"

He laughed and opened his arms again. "How did you get so far away on the couch?"

She went to him. And he cradled her for a long time. Neither feeling the need for words.

There was no place she'd rather be. For the first time in her life, she'd truly found home.

The next few weeks flew by. Will and Maddox spent a lot of time with Kara. He couldn't help but notice Soufflé seemed to have acquired a great many more toys. And his own name-inscribed, porcelain feeding bowl.

Will rolled his eyes at her. "Why do I get the feeling that even when the splint comes off, that cat is going nowhere?"

She laughed. "No more strays."

They cooked dinner together almost every evening at her house. He'd certainly never eaten better. And his heart had never felt so full. Maddox blossomed under her nurturing presence. Will began to imagine if those sweet times never had to end.

Which scared him. But taking courage from Kara's past,

he soldiered through. Determined to relish every ounce of happiness while he could.

His perspective glass half-empty, he couldn't quite shake the sense—based on past experience—that it wouldn't last. Nothing good ever did.

The council vote kept getting kicked down the road. But finally it was scheduled for the Thursday before Easter. Still a few weeks away.

He tried not to dwell on it. Or agonize over what the outcome might be. Instead, he focused on doing his job, being a good dad and spending as much time as humanly possible off the clock with Kara.

Yet, always at the back of his mind, the impending decision loomed large. Change was a fact of life. But change never brought him anything good. He resolved to not try to look too far ahead, but to enjoy the now.

The Saturday morning of the Flapjack Flip-Off dawned. Standing outside the open firehouse bay, he had an excellent vantage point for observing the proceedings on the square.

ErmaJean was the president of the ladies' auxiliary, and her helpers had been busy. Miss IdaLee, who'd taught at least three generations of Truelovers, had used all her connections to secure some great raffle prizes this year. Lila Penry's art students had designed the colorful fliers Luke, Zach and the other guys hung around town.

GeorgeAnne had been less than thrilled at the direction this year's fund-raiser had taken, but Will was about done with her muleheadedness. If she didn't like it, she could boycott the Flip-Off. And miss out on all the fun, too.

The ROMEO component—Callie's dad, Amber's dad, Maggie's dad and Pops among others—had been in charge of the layout. Foldout tables and chairs lay scattered across the green for diners. The two competing griddles were deployed on either side of the gazebo.

The café was temporarily shuttered for today's event. An event he hoped would bring the community together in support of Kara. And the other downtown businesses would enjoy a red-letter day, reaping the benefits of the Flip-Off. Including GeorgeAnne's hardware store.

His gaze skimmed over the blonde chef who arrived at 6:30 a.m. to set up her station. The competition would begin at eight sharp.

In a matching black chef's coat, Leo would flip crêpes alongside Kara. Shayla and Trudy were working the fixin's on the side. Crêpe lovers could choose between savory fillings or sweet toppings, like fresh whipped cream, chocolate sauce or a maple-pecan syrup.

Will had a quiet word with Shayla about surreptitiously saving him some of both. His public loyalty had to shine forth for the TFD. But privately?

His stomach belonged to Kara.

As for his heart? He scrubbed his face with his hand. He headed over to check on Zach and the guys manning the pancake side of the competition.

Family-friendly interactive opportunities would begin at nine, including a demo of an aerial ladder rescue and a tour of the firehouse. Unless called out, the apparatus would be on display for the kids to climb into for a photo op.

A sizable crowd gathered underneath the tall, stately oaks. Mayor Watson mounted the steps to the gazebo. He tapped the mic. At the electronic blare, everyone flinched.

Will took his place on the platform as the TFD representative. His gaze roaming over familiar faces, he estimated at least two hundred people had shown up to support the worthy cause. He hoped town council members were taking notice.

Mayor Watson made a few general remarks and then got to the reason they'd gathered. "All you can eat until eleven a.m." He chuckled. Underneath the husky-sized, red golf shirt, his round belly jiggled. Come December, the mayor doubled for Santa. "Don't want any of you leaving hungry."

"No fear of that," Tom Arledge, Pops's best friend, shouted and patted his lean belly. "I'm here to do my part."

Everyone laughed.

"This year we have a special addition. A real sweet treat with the Mason Jar's own Kara Lockwood." Mayor Watson's blue eyes twinkled. "Crêpes or pancakes. Don't forget to vote for your favorite by putting the suggested donation of five or ten dollars into either the boot—" he gestured at the leather firefighter boot on the table in front of Zach's crew "—or the hat."

Kara had upturned a chef's hat on her table.

"The team with the most donations at the end of the day wins. It's breakfast, it's a contest and it's a fund-raiser." Mayor Watson fingered his white beard. "What could be more fun?"

Will spotted the missing member of the matchmaker trifecta at the back of the crowd. He bit back a smile. Sure enough, GeorgeAnne hadn't been able to resist attending.

"Lady and gentlemen." The mayor's jolly, broad face broke into a grin. He winked, playing to the crowd. "You see what I did there?"

Will fought the urge to exchange glances with Kara.

"On your mark, get set…griddle!" the mayor yelled.

And the competition commenced.

Kara and Leo went to work. As did Zach and Lieutenant Bradley. Spatulas flashed in the sunshine of the April morning. A delicious steam rose off both grills. And there was a whole lot of flipping going on.

Looked like Pops had organized the small fry of Truelove into a cheering section. The Green girls, Maddox and his best buds, the Hollingsworth boys, Maisie McAbee, Jonas's mini-me cowboy Hunter and sweet little Emma Cate Gibson.

The TFD had their own supporters, as well.

Arms folded, the barbecue queen stood off to the side, her lips curled in a soft smile at the small-town antics.

Within minutes each team sported stacks of completed product. Lines formed quickly. The light, golden-brown hues of the crêpes and pancakes were a pretty sight to behold.

Alongside toppings of cinnamon apple, powdered sugar and a mix of berries, Trudy dished out her brand of sassy ribbing. Even the fire crew couldn't help but laugh.

Kara remained focused and calm. Completely in her element. Her cheeks rosy from the heat off the griddle. Her blue eyes sparkled.

But he was nervous enough for the both of them. Behind the scenes, he was unable to stop pacing. Totally thrilled as Kara's line grew longer and longer. People returned for second and third helpings.

Watching her work, so poised, he couldn't help reflect on what she'd shared with him about her childhood. Every time he thought of it, it made his chest contract and his gut knot. At all she'd gone through and so young. It made him admire her all the more for what she'd accomplished as an acclaimed, award-winning chef.

He also recognized her willingness to open her heart to him had been a gift. A gift she didn't share with many. A privilege afforded to him. And a responsibility.

She made him feel something he'd never felt before. For the first time since the fiasco with Liz, he wondered if God would give him a second chance at love.

Perhaps God hadn't cast him aside. Perhaps this time a

relationship was possible. He found himself believing that his future might be bright with promise.

Mayor Watson called a halt at eleven. By eleven thirty, the local accounting firm of Penry and Penry were ready to announce the results.

All total, the event raked in over three thousand dollars. Loud gasps punctuated the throng. Will could hardly believe it, either. This was the largest take of any previous Truelove fund-raiser for the Firefighter Cancer Foundation.

Myra Penry, Lila's mother, stepped up to the mic. "And I am also pleased to declare the winner of Truelove's first-ever Flapjack Flip-Off…" She grinned at the crowd, letting the suspense mount.

He clenched his fists at his sides. Afraid to breathe.

"By only a slim margin… It was close, ladies and gentlemen." Myra held aloft the gold-plated spatula trophy. "But the winner is…"

Please, God, I know it's been a long time. But for Kara's sake… He closed his eyes.

"Kara Lockwood and team!"

His eyes flew open. Leo caught his petite boss in a bear hug, lifting her off her feet and whirling her around. The crowd went wild. Stomping and clapping.

Including the members of his fire brigade. Because Kara's food was just that good. Earlier, he'd caught Zach stuffing his face with one of the strawberry and whipped cream crêpes.

He shot a glance over the crowd, locating GeorgeAnne. A begrudging smile hovered on her face, too.

Then he focused on Kara's lovely, laughing, flushed features. Suddenly, more than anything in the world, he wanted to kiss her. And before the day was out, he resolved to do just that.

But with the event winding down, he had to make sure

the firehouse was set to rights first. A small-town fire chief was never really off duty. Pops and Miss Glorieta disappeared somewhere with Maddox.

He went around checking on his guys. Shaking their hands. Offering halfhearted commiseration, but sincere appreciation to Zach and the crew.

The men took their defeat good-naturedly. He glimpsed in Zach and company new respect for the French-loving chef. And Will was filled with such hope. Such certainty that Kara was right. That God would work everything out for their good.

Surely, the council would acknowledge the TFD's essential role in the community. His relationship with Kara would have the freedom to flourish. And Maddox…

Will set off across the deserted green to congratulate Kara at the Mason Jar.

His son might eventually acquire a cream-colored tabby with a love of soufflés. And one day Maddox might even Will's heart skipped a beat—get a mother to call his own.

A few long strides brought him to the entrance. With a quick jerk, he thrust open the door. At the sound of the bell, Kara turned. She'd placed her trophy beside the little silver Eiffel Tower.

She smiled at him, and he thought his heart might burst in two. Her smile was like the sun coming out from behind the clouds, after decades of dreary rain.

Cupping her elbows in his hands, he lifted her off her feet.

"Will—oh," she gasped.

He carried her to his favorite red swivel stool and set her down. "I'm so proud of you."

"Thank you," she murmured.

He felt her breath on his cheek. His heart pounded. Did

she feel what he felt for her? An enormous, knee-buckling, overwhelming tide of rightness.

"Can I kiss you?" he rasped.

"I thought you'd never ask." The blue in her eyes deepened to indigo. "Please. Do."

He brushed his mouth over hers. Giving her the chance to pull away if she chose. But she didn't.

She wrapped her arms around his neck. And the next kiss was hers. His sassy, independent, give-as-good-as-she-got chef.

Now at long last, spring had unfurled in his heart. Forever throwing off winter's chill. Nevermore to return.

As if by unspoken, unanimous consent, they both came up for air. Unwilling to let her drift far, however, he held her in his arms. His chest heaved. His heart thundered.

Clapping broke out on the other side of the cut-through window.

Looking over Kara's shoulder, he realized they'd had an audience, but he didn't care. Leo ducked his head, and Shayla blushed.

"Woo-hoo!" Trudy heckled. "'Bout time, you two."

Glorieta and Pops grinned.

Wearing the ever-present plastic firefighter helmet, Maddox fist-pumped the air. "Way to go, Daddy!"

Chuckling, Will rested his forehead against Kara's.

"You kiss pretty good. For a fire chief," she whispered.

He pressed his lips against her smooth skin. "You aren't too bad yourself."

"This time *I'm* asking for a rain check." Her lovely gaze flickered from their friends and family. "Without the rubberneckers."

He twined his fingers through hers. "Say the word and I'll be there." A call to which he'd be delighted to respond.

Anytime. Anyplace. Anywhere.

Chapter Nine

Over the next couple of weeks Kara realized she'd been going about fitting into Truelove all wrong. And she made the necessary adjustments to correct course.

Each day more petition-signing customers returned. Since her Flip-Off victory, the word about Kara's cooking had spread. Will had been right.

The kiss at the Mason Jar was the stuff that dreams were made of. The memory brought a heated tint of pink to her cheeks. And though Will continued to be under a great deal of stress with the fate of the TFD hanging over him, it was by no means the only kiss they shared over subsequent days.

It was a struggle to keep her mind on the café. She was more or less successful, depending on how long since she'd seen him last.

Dwight Fleming, owner of a local rafting company and Amber's father, was the first of the ROMEOs to make a sheepish reappearance. "My wife told me I could either get over it or find other living accommodations, such as the doghouse."

By the next day the ROMEO breakfast club was back in

full swing. In the booth with his old friends, Pops raised his café au lait to her in a toast.

Kara, Lila and her mom, Myra, finalized reception food details. The cooking videos on Heart's Home had found a growing audience. Callie hired her to cater Amber's baby shower.

Through her landlady, Wilda Arledge, Kara connected with an agency that delivered weekly meals to shut-ins. She always had leftover food so she began dropping off the extra at the firehouse. And when she discovered there was a soup kitchen located nearby at the county seat, a charity near and dear to her heart, she volunteered to supply a meal once a week.

One afternoon Maggie talked her into giving her boys and Maddox a short cooking class after the café closed for the day. It was so much fun, she decided to do it again the next week. This time she knew better what to expect for their age level.

She and Glorieta made a quick trip to the big-box craft store on the highway at the outlet mall. And she had tiny chef hats with their names embroidered—Miss IdaLee had taken care of that—and small aprons for them, as well.

Maggie and her mother-in-law, Wilda, supervised Austin and Logan while Glorieta oversaw Maddox. Leaving Kara free to teach.

"Would you consider teaching a couple of classes during the summer session at the rec center?" Maggie pushed the hat away from Austin's eyes. His tongue sticking out of his mouth, he concentrated on spooning the cherry filling into the dough-lined muffin tin. "Lila says Emma Cate is dying to try out her culinary skills."

"Classy Kids Cook?" Kara cocked her head, a slow smile spreading across her face. "I love the idea. Sign me up."

"Uh, Maggie?" Wilda pointed to Logan. He had more cherry filling on his hands and face than appeared to have made it to the tart shells.

Each of them holding an arm high, Kara and Maggie escorted Logan to the sink. Climbing the stool, he thrust his hands under the flowing water and soaped up.

"Since the petition incident, your aunt GeorgeAnne hasn't been to the restaurant." Kara bit her lip. "I didn't mean for her to feel barred for life."

It surprised Kara how much she felt the older lady's absence. It was weird seeing the two Double Name Club members seated at their usual table near the bulletin board minus their sharp-tongued de facto leader. But Kara didn't know how to make that right.

Maggie made sure Logan lathered between his fingers. "Change is harder for some than others."

Bringing Will to Kara's mind.

"I also discovered that Walter went away to stay with his daughter over the winter."

A retired judge, Walter was GeorgeAnne's not-so-secret gentleman friend.

Maggie handed a drying cloth to her son. "Walter hasn't come back, and I think Aunt GeorgeAnne is afraid he never will. I think Walter's absence was the real tipping point that sent my aunt into orbit. The hardware store is doing better."

Which Kara was thrilled to hear. It was hard to be a small business owner. Especially in the current economy. She bore the Allen clan no animosity.

Maggie took Logan's hand as he climbed down from the step stool. "I know it was you, Kara, who suggested AnnaBeth do a feature on GeorgeAnne and the store."

Kara fluttered her hands. "It was no big deal."

"But it was. It gave the store the shot in the arm it

needed with publicity. My cousins, GeorgeAnne's sons, somehow also managed to override her objections to adding an online component to the store, emphasizing its old-fashioned, small-town appeal. Business has picked up. I think the worst is over."

"Good news."

"Thanks in large part to you shoving my aunt in the right direction."

Just then the oven dinged, signaling the first batch of cherry tartlets was ready to be removed. The children watched from their stools at the prep station as she took the tins out of the oven. After the mini-pies cooled, they celebrated by eating them. Plus, a generous scoop of vanilla ice cream.

That evening Glorieta took Kara out for a surprise dinner.

"Monday is Terence's daughter's birthday."

"How could I have forgotten?" Kara laid down her fork. "And of course, you must be there."

She'd become so used to Glorieta as part of the Mason Jar team, she'd almost forgotten Mama G had other responsibilities at home.

"The restaurant seems to have turned a corner."

Oh, how Kara hoped so.

"I won't be gone forever." Glorieta reached across the table and laid her hand over Kara's. "I'll be back. You can't get rid of me that easy, missy."

Kara refused to allow herself to cry. She'd known this day had to come. She would just miss the stout-hearted woman so much.

Blinking rapidly, she lifted her chin. "I wish I could be there this year. Tell Meriah happy birthday for me. I promise to make a trip to Durham next Sunday when the Jar's closed and celebrate with her, albeit belatedly."

"Thinking about bringing a certain fire chief and his adorable son?"

Unable to hide her smile, she beamed at her foster mother. "Do you think I should?"

Mama G nodded. "Seems like it's getting serious. You two have spent a lot of time together since the contest. What has he said to you about his feelings?"

Kara ran her tongue over her teeth. Actually, not much. But that was her solemn, keeps-his-feelings-close Will.

"He has trust issues. And a lot of baggage to overcome."

Glorieta didn't say anything, but her gaze never wavered from Kara.

She twisted the napkin in her lap. "He's cautious by nature. Which is what makes him such a great leader and fire chief. And after that woman—"

"His ex-wife."

Kara winced. "After she did a number on his head… He has to reason things through for himself. Consider the implications for Maddox. And of course, he's distracted about the ongoing turmoil over the TFD."

She was aware she was rambling. And making excuses?

"What do you want out of this relationship with Will, Kara? How do you see your future unfolding?"

"You and I both know the restaurant business can be all-consuming."

Glorieta propped her elbow on the tabletop. "So how do Will and his son figure into your plans?"

"I want a life outside the café, which is one of the reasons I was drawn to buying this property in the first place." Kara leaned forward. "Open only for breakfast and lunch. Closing each day in time for me to be there after school for my children. With nights free to enjoy my family."

Glorieta nodded.

"As for my business plans?" Kara opened her hands.

"Best-case scenario, the Mason Jar does so well I can hire a manager to take over day-to-day operations. Surprisingly, I think with some training, Trudy would be perfect for the job. Leaving me free to do what I really love."

Glorieta pursed her lips. "Cooking."

Kara placed her hands on either side of her plate. "And since we're brainstorming here, one day I'd love to contract the pastries out. Truelove needs its own bakery, which maybe I'd co-own. And if the sky's the limit on dreaming, I'd add a more upscale haute cuisine restaurant for evening diners?"

"Big dreams. And why not?" Glorieta's smile widened. "Your own Truelove restaurant empire."

"Above all else, I see Will and Maddox in my life." Kara sat back in her chair. "I can't imagine any of it—I wouldn't want any of it—unless they were there, too."

Please, God. Let it be so.

God's purposes were always for good. So much had changed for her since moving to Truelove. She'd found a life she hadn't imagined could be hers. A home.

Is this what You intended all along for me, God?

Her feelings for Will so new and real, she was almost too afraid to even verbalize them. Time to stop hiding behind her fears that it couldn't last. That this, like so many other things she'd loved, was too good to be true. Too good to last.

Time to stop waiting for the other shoe to drop. Time to embrace and enjoy all the blessings God had wrought for her in this small mountain town.

She'd never been so happy. And it was all because of a small-town fire chief and his adorable son.

With the town council vote scheduled for late afternoon, Will decided to get his Kara and chocolate croissant fix a little earlier than usual on Thursday. He strolled inside and took a seat on a stool at the counter.

Trudy wandered over his way. "I'm assuming you want the VIP treatment from the boss?" she said with a smirk.

Will laughed. "If she's available."

Trudy rolled her eyes. "Don't see her ever being too busy to spend time with you." She pushed at the porthole door. "I'll get her."

He did a quick scan of the front area dining room. A few lunch patrons still lingered. He waved to Jake and his father-in-law, Nash, probably on a supply run for the orchard.

The kitchen door swung open and Kara glided through. "Hey, stranger. Long time, no see."

Will grinned.

He and Maddox had dinner at Kara's just last night. She'd pulled out her collection of ceramic mixing bowls. Vivid reds, blues and yellows, all the way from France. He'd flinched a little every time she let Maddox near the matching prep bowls. But his son had a blast helping put together the tacos—the French-inspired tacos.

And thankfully, nothing was damaged in the making of dinner.

"With Glorieta back in Durham, I didn't want you to get lonely."

"That's very considerate of you," she said.

He lifted his chin. "I'm a very considerate guy."

"Yes, you are." She batted her eyes at him. "Among other things." She handed him a menu. "Time for that rain check."

"I thought I might be out of rain checks by now."

"Nope. Take a look at the dessert page."

"But I usually just—"

"Will MacKenzie." She tapped her foot on the linoleum. "Look at the dessert page."

"Yes, ma'am." He scanned the listings. So fun to push her buttons. Get her all riled—

"Whoa." He looked up. "You put the apple pie back on the menu."

"I did." She sniffed. "Right beside my apple tart galette."

He leaned against the stool. "Good for you."

"I decided Truelove was big enough for both desserts."

He smiled. "I agree."

She pretended to take an imaginary order pad from her skirt pocket. "So what will it be today, Chief MacKenzie?"

"I think I'm going to take a walk on the French side." He hiked his brows. "The galette, if you please." He handed over the menu. "See if it lives up to the hype."

"Oh, it will." She gave him a look. "I promise you, it will."

He moistened his lips. "Looking forward to it."

After placing his order, she returned, propping her arms on the counter. "What's my favorite firefighter-in-training up to today?"

"Pops took him to the dollar store. Somehow over the last year, his Easter basket got lost so they've gone to replace it."

"Ah. The egg hunt on the square tomorrow." She shook her head. "I can't believe it's almost Easter."

He waggled his eyebrows. "Stick with me, kid, and I'll make sure you've got a front-row seat to all the big events in Truelove."

"I look forward to seeing you there."

He hunched his shoulders. "By then, I guess I'll know one way or the other about the station. Being in limbo is the worst."

Leo dinged the bell.

Kara whirled toward the pass-through window. "You know what *stressed* spells backward, right?" She set the plate before him as if bestowing crown jewels. *"Desserts."*

At the aromatic steam rising off the hot apple tart, his nose twitched in appreciation. "Here goes." He stuck his fork into the slice, speared off a segment and brought it to his mouth.

Her gaze fastened on his.

Will closed his lips and chewed. His eyes widened. "Wow." He took another bite.

"As good as advertised?"

"Better." He swallowed. "Tastes almost as good as you look."

A becoming shade of rose pink blossomed in her cheeks. He loved that she was a woman who still blushed. And that he could cause her to do so.

Her eyes sparkled. "The galette must be mighty good, then," she teased.

"It is."

They made plans to meet again that evening. A real date this time. Just the two of them.

He glanced at the clock above the chalkboard specials. "I should go. I want to go over my closing argument one more time before the council hearing. Pray for me?"

Reaching over, she squeezed his hand. "Always."

He climbed off the stool. "If there weren't all these people here, I'd give you a proper kiss right now."

"I don't recall it stopping you last time."

He laughed. "You are very good for me, Kara Lockwood. But so much of a distraction. Rain check, okay?"

She grinned. "That tab of yours keeps adding up."

Unable to resist her any further, he leaned over and planted a quick kiss on her upturned face. "Tonight." He sighed. "What is it that makes your food so much better than anyone else's?"

"I have a secret ingredient." She smiled. "Everything I make is made with love."

Two hours later he found himself whistling as he walked over to the town hall. But the afternoon went downhill fast. Despite his and Bridger's impassioned pleas, the council voted to shut down the TFD.

Afterward, Bridger looked about as stunned as Will felt. "I'm so sorry, man."

They parted ways on the sidewalk outside the town hall.

Will looked across the square to the station. The fire department had been his world for as long as he could remember. There were not enough available slots at the larger county firehouse to absorb the entire TFD.

How could he face his men? What was his crew going to do now? Will rubbed his throbbing temples. What was *he* going to do now?

The Roebuck fire chief would have no need of another chief in his own firehouse. Will found himself in the unenviable position of being overqualified and undervalued.

He could pretty much count on a demotion. If he was even able to secure a job at another fire station. A big *if*. His entire career might be over. And if he didn't work for a fire department, what else would he do?

What else could he do?

But no matter which way he looked at it, relocating was an absolute given.

Maddox would be distraught at the prospect of moving away from his best buds, Austin and Logan. When Will had been so alone and Maddox's life so precarious, Pops had given up everything for them—his career, his home, his town.

And now when Pops had finally won his battle against cancer, and found his place in Truelove with the ROMEOs again, how could Will ask him to throw it all away?

He couldn't. Pain exploded behind his eyelids. He just couldn't.

Somehow, he found himself standing in front of the Mason Jar. Late-afternoon light dappled the sidewalk. The diner was closed.

Where was Kara? His gut knotted. She was probably in the kitchen, baking for tomorrow's menu. Unaware that everything had changed. Nothing could be the same. Not for him. Not for them.

This was the end of everything.

He could hardly believe only a few hours ago he'd felt as if life held so much hope. That finally, after the sorrow, the disillusionment, the loneliness…

Will raked his hand over his head. What a chump he'd been to think his future would be bright with promise. Liz, God, the town council—he'd been cast aside again.

There. Were. No. Second. Chances.

At least, not for him. He was a failure. As a husband. As a son. As a fire chief. And knowing what else he needed to do, soon he'd be a failure as a father, too. Denying Maddox access to the one person he wanted above all else.

Will refused to stand in the way of Kara's dreams. She could do nothing to change the fact that he'd lost his job or that he was going to have to move away from Truelove. Her life, her dream, however, was firmly planted in the mountain soil of the sleepy Blue Ridge town.

He'd never dream of making her choose. He wouldn't ask her to give up anything for him. Because if she did, he'd eventually fail her, too.

And that was more than he could bear. To see the special thing between them unravel. The disappointment in her eyes when she looked at him. The resentment of what being with him had cost her. The both of them forced to reenact the animosity he'd experienced with Liz.

He couldn't do it. Will gritted his teeth. More than that, he wouldn't do it. Not to Kara. Not to Maddox. Not ever again.

She'd been such a gift to him and Maddox. It had been a privilege to know her. And because he lov—no, not that.

He didn't do love. But because he'd felt something for her that he'd not felt for anyone before, he had a responsibility to make sure he didn't ruin her.

Before he could change his mind, he yanked open the door. The bell jangled. Kara popped her head around the swinging door.

"Hey, you." Dimples bracketed her cheeks. "Couldn't wait until tonight to see me again, huh?" She smiled.

And suddenly, he was so angry. So angry at Liz, at God, at the council, at himself.

He scowled. "I've told you a hundred times not to leave that door unlocked when you're here all alone."

Kara's smile fell. "What's wrong?" She bridged the distance between them. "What's happened?"

"The Truelove Fire Department is closing. Effective June first."

She gasped. "Oh, Will. I'm so sorry." She took hold of his arm. "I'm—"

He jerked away. She put her hand to her throat.

If she touched him, he was done for. He'd be lost. Unable to do what he came to do. Walk away from her and everything he'd been foolish enough to believe was possible for him.

"Maddox and I will have to relocate."

"Okay." She lifted her chin. "We can work with that. We'll find a way to work around that." His brave, spunky Kara.

If he only possessed an ounce of the courage she had in spades...

"You're not listening to me." He scrubbed his face. "It's

no good. You and me. There's no use in prolonging the inevitable."

"You don't mean that." Tears pooled in those lovely blueberry eyes of hers. "You're just upset. You're not thinking clearly. I love you, Will."

"Don't say that to me," he growled. "I don't do love, Kara." He scoured his mouth with his hand.

She flinched.

"One day you'll thank me."

Tears rolled down her cheeks. The pain in her eyes—pain he was inflicting—stabbed him in his heart.

"That's not true," she whispered. "What we've felt for each other… Please don't do this." Desperation flickered across her face.

He was so weary. So tired. And sad.

"You deserve so much more than someone like me." He dropped his gaze, unable to bear the anguish on her face. "It's over, Kara." He turned toward the door.

"Don't say that. Will. Please. Look at me."

But if he looked at her again, he'd never be able to leave her. "It's better this ends right now." He beheld his reflection and behind him, hers, too, in the glass-fronted door. And he hated himself for hurting her.

"If you could just manage to hang on a little while longer to your faith in us, in our future —"

"That's what I'm trying to tell you." Not turning around, he squared his shoulders. "I don't see a future for us. Not for you and me and Maddox."

She staggered and caught hold of the register.

He felt so hollowed out, empty. "Goodbye, Kara."

Will thrust open the door. And then he walked away.

To be the bearer of further bad tidings. Breaking the news to his men that they were all out of work.

Chapter Ten

At 3:00 a.m., lightning struck a barn at a farm just outside Truelove. And Will got the call to respond.

He hadn't been asleep. After walking away from Kara, sleep had proven impossible. But back at the house Friday morning, he was operating on fumes.

Bleary eyed, he hunched over a mug of freshly brewed coffee. He grimaced. Freshly brewed, boring, plain ole American coffee.

And he felt miserable. But once burned, twice shy. So why did he feel like he'd just made the biggest mistake of his life? He'd done the right thing. Hadn't he?

"Quite the storm." Pops shuffled into the kitchen. "I heard you pacing half the night before you got called out."

"Sorry," he grunted. "A lot on my mind."

When Will arrived home from the diner last night, his father had seen how distraught he was and forced him to come clean about what happened between him and Kara. Pops hadn't held back his views on what he thought about that.

Pops pulled out a chair and sat down. "Figured out yet how you're going to break the news to your son that you've cost him the best thing to ever come into your lives?"

He winced. "That's not fair. I'm trying to protect my son."

"From Kara?" Pops snorted. "Sure it's Maddox you're determined to protect and not yourself?"

He scraped his hand over his head. "I really don't need this from you."

Pops grunted. "Seems to me you don't think you need anything or anyone."

"I've lost my job. I've lost everyone's jobs."

Pops made a face. "The town council is responsible for closing the firehouse, Will, not you."

"Maybe if I'd fought harder. Said or done something different…"

"I don't think there was anything you could have said or done that would've changed the outcome of the council's vote." Pops grimaced. "Shortsighted is what it is. And I'm afraid someone is going to pay the price for their lack of vision. Probably won't be their house burning down, though."

Will scrubbed the back of his neck. "Bottom line remains I've gotta find work. And unfortunately, I'm going to have to relocate to do that."

"Still don't see what this has to do with Kara."

"How could there be a future for us?" Will threw out his hands. "Maddox and I could end up who knows where, but because of the Mason Jar, she's tied to Truelove."

Pops pursed his lips. "Kara is a real smart little gal. Did you even bother asking for her opinion?"

He frowned. "There's no point in asking."

Pops shook his head. "So as far as Kara is concerned, you just up and dumped her. Walked away. Like Liz walked away from you."

"I didn't…" Will clenched his jaw. "She's better off without me. I would've only held her back. I'm no good at relationships." He scrubbed his face. "I've failed at everything. As fire chief. With Liz—"

"You hold on right there, mister." Pops wagged his finger. "You need to stop feeling sorry for yourself and see sense. You did not fail this town. This town failed you. And as for Liz…"

His father's eyes glinted. Pops was the most mild-mannered of men. But he had no use for Will's ex-wife.

"Liz failed you and your son. That's on her. Not you. And what about Maddox? What about how he feels for Kara?"

Will swallowed. "He's young. He'll get over it. He'll move on."

"Like you've gotten over Liz? Like you've moved on from the divorce?" Pops jutted his jaw. "How has that worked out for you, son? Not so well. And here you are wishing a lifetime of that same kind of unhappiness on Maddox?"

"I got over Liz a long time ago, Pops." He gritted his teeth. "You don't know what you're talking about."

"Perhaps so. Maybe the real issue is not about forgiving Liz, but about forgiving yourself." His father's gaze bored into his. "And forgiving God for allowing the hurt into your life."

Will sucked in a breath.

"Letting go of your anger at Him over Liz. The trauma over Maddox's birth. Your mom's passing." His dad's eyes never left his. "My cancer."

"I'm not…" He bit back the words. He was angry. He'd been angry for a long time. Truth was, the anger was far better than the hollowness he too often felt inside.

"Until you make peace with yourself and God, son—" his father's gaze grew sad "—the emptiness will follow you wherever you go. And you'll never find the happiness you so desperately want."

"I—I can't." He turned his face. "I'm not ready." He might never be.

"Stubborn is what you are."

Just then, his phone started beeping. So much for being off duty on Good Friday.

"Aren't you and Tom Arledge going fishing today?" Will rose. "I was supposed to take Maddox to the Easter egg hunt this afternoon. Would you call Miss ErmaJean and see if she could take him instead?"

Pops folded his arms. "I'll do that, but tonight we need to finish talking through this, son."

"I'm finished in Truelove, Pops." He squared his shoulders. "Maddox and I will be relocating. We'd love to have you join us. But you have a life in Truelove, and if you'd prefer to remain here, I understand."

His father's Adam's apple bobbed.

"I'm done talking, Pops." He pushed back his chair. "If you choose to come with us, I don't want to ever have this conversation again. Are we clear?"

"One way or the other, son, God will find a way to get your attention." The older man let out a long, drawn-out breath. "No doubt about it."

The call turned out to be a multivehicle pileup on the interstate. Bridger and his officers were already on scene when Will pulled his SUV onto the side of the highway. His crew and the TFD engine rolled in seconds behind him. EMTs from all over the county were working the incident. Several occupants were trapped inside their cars and needed assistance.

Quickly assessing the emergency, he deployed his troops to where they could do the most good. He kept in radio contact with Dispatch and monitored the situation. After a while Bridger joined him beside the engine.

Zach used the Jaws of Life to cut through the steel to rescue a woman trapped behind the wheel of her red sedan. The grinding buzz set Will's teeth on edge. Luke and Bradley extricated the woman. Paramedics transferred her to a gurney. His crew moved on to the next victim.

"It started with a truck hydroplaning." Rain dripped off the brim of Bridger's regulation hat. "The driver crashed into the guardrail. Chain reaction after that."

The two men gazed the length of the highway. Traffic was backed up for miles in both directions. No one was going anywhere fast. And the rain continued to pour.

It hadn't been raining when he left Truelove. But that was the way it was in the Blue Ridge. Dry in the valley, but a storm on the mountain. Or vice versa.

"Hope nobody needs fire or police in Truelove," Bridger remarked, only half joking.

Will made a face. "If they're on fire, they better get used to calling the county station."

They headed in opposite directions to offer their assistance to ongoing rescue efforts. An hour later the TFD had done everything they could. The ambulances were off, en route to the small regional hospital.

But Bridger and his officers would be on scene a while yet. To take statements and unsnarl traffic.

Will was helping his guys load the last of their equipment when Zach frowned at something in the distance.

"Uh, Chief?" Zach's face paled. "We've got another, bigger problem, I think."

He closed the storage compartment on the rig with a bang. "What's that?"

Zach's bony finger pointed and Will turned. For a split

second, the crew stopped what they were doing to stare. Mouths ajar. Horror fixed on their features.

On the horizon, a dark cloud had engulfed the top of the mountain range. Lightning crackled. Thunder roared. Out of the angry black sky, a whitish funnel appeared.

The monster dipped and swayed. Racing over the ridge. Debris billowed in its wake. Destroying everything in its path.

And on the other side of the mountain…

"Truelove," Luke whispered.

Will's temporary paralysis broke. "Get in the vehicles!" he shouted, running for the SUV. "Go! Go! Go!" he yelled over his shoulder.

The firefighters scrambled into the rig. Inside the SUV, he sent out a warning for Dispatch to send out a distress call to the larger county station and for additional emergency personnel. But on a day like this, resources were stretched thin. Who knew if anyone else could respond?

Barreling toward town, he prayed. For the safety of everyone in the path of the devouring beast. For the town that had fired him. For his family and friends.

For Kara.

But mostly that he wasn't already too late to help them.

In the lull after lunch, Kara sat at her desk in the tiny office tallying the day's receipts.

The culinary opinion tide in Truelove was slowly turning her way. Her food was winning hearts and appetites. The café was holding its own. Her bottom line was looking up.

Catering the Penry-Gibson wedding reception would put her numbers in the plus column next month. Expanding her operation to include a catering service opened up all kinds of intriguing and potentially lucrative possibilities.

Kara might be slightly down, but she definitely wasn't out. Despite GeorgeAnne's interference, she had the strong support of the Mason Jar regulars. And her patronage was growing.

She should've been ecstatic about the café, but losing Will and Maddox left her feeling hopeless, her victory hollow.

Kara rubbed her throbbing temples. She fumbled through her desk drawer until she found the pain relief bottle she kept there. She'd battled the dull ache in her head since she got up this morning.

After Will's rejection at the café yesterday, in a stupor she'd dragged herself home and cried until she had no tears left. Last night's thunderstorm kept her awake for hours. Curling up against her side, Soufflé had proven a comforting presence.

Once when she and her mom were homeless, they were caught out in a storm on the streets with nowhere to go for shelter. And she'd never quite overcome her deep-seated fear of storms.

It didn't have to be a big one, either. She understood the fear was irrational. But even a few rumbles in the middle of the night sent her burrowing under the covers, a cringing shell of her usually confident self.

Leaving her computer, she went into the kitchen to get a glass of water. The kitchen put to rights, Leo had already left for the day. Standing at the sink, she downed the pain reliever capsules. In the front dining room, Shayla and Trudy were finishing up their cleaning protocols for closing.

Trudy poked her bottle-blonde, heavily lacquered head through the cut-out window. "Good day for the till?"

She forced a smile. "A good day."

The waitress pursed her lips. "Feels like we've turned a corner, don't you think?"

We've. Success, hard-won, felt great. Loyalty felt better.

"Definitely a team effort." Kara touched her arm. "I couldn't have done it without you, Trudy."

Instead of elation, however, she felt barely able to function. She'd been on autopilot all day. Just going through the motions.

And it seemed as if every major crisis of her life had to involve bystanders. GeorgeAnne's ultimatum. The kiss. Losing Will.

Waiting for Zach's auto body shop to finish the inspection on her car, Trudy had been hanging out with Kara in the kitchen when Will had arrived yesterday afternoon.

Trudy had overheard every word. And in her distress, Kara had discovered that there was far more to the hip-swinging waitress. It had been Trudy who rushed to her side when Will walked away. And she made sure Kara got home in one piece.

"Come see, Miss Kara." Shayla stood at the window overlooking the square. "Maddox is lined up on the steps of the gazebo with the other little boys for the bow tie contest."

Because she couldn't resist Will's son, Kara hurried into the dining area.

The sun shone in a blue sky, but it remained slightly blustery. Since it was Good Friday, school was out for spring break and most of the downtown businesses were closed. But a smallish crowd of doting grandmas and moms had convened under the oaks on the square to participate in the annual Truelove Easter Egg Hunt.

Kara glanced across the green toward the fire station. The bay was empty. It had been an active twenty-four hours for the TFD. Will and his crew must have been called out again.

She looked for Pops, but didn't see him. And then she remembered his date with a fish. Her head throbbed. A combination of sorrow, and perhaps a change in barometric pressure. When she lost Will, she not only lost Maddox but Pops, too. Like a stone tossed in a pond, the ripple effects continued to widen.

It made her sad to think of no longer being in his life. For a too-short, deliriously happy time she'd believed she was meant to be Maddox's mother. And Rick MacKenzie had quickly become the father figure she'd longed for but barely recalled after the early death of her own dad.

ErmaJean must've brought Maddox to the festivities. Tom's twin grandsons, Austin and Logan, stood on either side of Maddox. Per her nature, GeorgeAnne was running the show. Mayor Watson handed out ribbons to the contest winners.

Maddox must've been watching for her. Catching sight of Kara in the window, his entire countenance lifted. He waved enthusiastically. Will must not have told the little boy yet about leaving Truelove. Nor about their broken relationship. It gutted her to think of never again being a part of Maddox's life.

Shayla grinned. "Isn't that Maddox MacKenzie just the cutest thing?"

His tan cap at a jaunty angle—*beret, thank you very much, Will MacKenzie*—Maddox truly was. The judges must've thought so, too. Last week she and Miss Erma-Jean had put together his wardrobe in anticipation of the contest. Khaki shorts, a button-down white shirt, tan suspenders and a red bow tie.

Of course, the original plan was for her and Will to bring him to the egg hunt together. So many plans, so many dreams that would never come true. She blinked back the sudden moisture welling up in her eyes. She was so sick of tears. And there appeared to be no end to her waterworks.

Shayla grabbed Kara's sleeve. "He won first place, Miss Kara."

Even from across the square, she could see the wide grin on her sweetie pie's face.

"And would you lookee there." Trudy joined them at the window. "The girls have on the sweetest little Easter bonnets."

Kara spotted Amber on the sidelines as Lucy and Stella paraded around in their ribbon-bedecked white straw hats. Emma Cate waved to her soon-to-be mommy, Lila. On photography duty, Callie McAbee watched proudly as her daughter Maisie received first place in the bonnet division.

A sudden gust of wind riffled the leafed-out oaks and sent Hunter Stone's cowboy hat careening into the bushes. He dashed after it. Next on the agenda—the egg hunt. The older children helped the smaller ones like Austin, Logan and Maddox locate the hidden eggs on the green.

She would dearly love to snap a photo of Maddox in his Easter outfit. But she hesitated, casting a glance over her shoulder to the office. And then there was the issue with Will…

"They're only little such a short time." Trudy patted her hand. "The receipts can wait. Our babies won't."

She blushed. "Maddox isn't my baby." Pain stabbed her heart. And he never would be.

Trudy's heavily plucked eyebrows hitched. "Maybe not right this minute, but I've seen how his daddy looks at you."

"Not anymore, Trudy."

Trudy shook her head. "He was upset about the fire station. He didn't mean those things he said. He'll change his mind. And I don't think it's any secret how you feel about Chief MacKenzie."

Kara brushed angry tears from her cheeks. "It doesn't matter how I feel, Trudy. They're moving as soon as Will gets another job."

So much had changed for her since coming to True-love. She'd found a life she hadn't imagined could be hers. A home.

All to have it snatched away. Perhaps she'd been better off not imagining. Not giving in to hope. Not allowing love to have its way with her heart.

But better off never knowing Maddox? She swallowed. No, she'd never regret knowing that sweet little boy. The child she'd so wanted to call her own.

"They haven't left yet, though." Trudy lifted her chin. "There's still today. And I think you should seize it."

She looked at Trudy. This might be her last chance to see Maddox. "Will probably doesn't want me—"

"Will isn't here." Trudy jutted her jaw. "And you are. What's one photo?"

The last photo she might ever get of Maddox. One photo to last her entire life. Years down the road, one final memory to recall the spring of her greatest happiness. When her heart had been full for the love of a man and his son.

She headed toward the door. "I won't be long."

Kara wasn't sure why, but she grabbed up the tiny Eiffel Tower beside the register and stuck it in her pocket.

On the distant horizon, the sun had gone behind a dark bank of clouds. Looked like there was weather on the mountain. The past few days had been unsettled. But hopefully, the children would get their egg hunt between rainstorms.

Trudy grabbed a mop. "I'm in no hurry. Shayla and I can finish here."

Kara crossed into the square. The wind picked up, blowing her hair into her eyes. Maddox ran to hug her. And she was glad she'd taken the time to walk over. GeorgeAnne gave her a baleful glare.

She snapped a few pics of Maddox with Austin and Logan. Maggie waved, but then her boys dragged her off in search of eggs. Clutching his basket, Maddox tore after his pals.

On her way back to the restaurant, she heard a distant rumble of thunder. She darted a look over her shoulder at the square. The crowd had dispersed. Parents rounded up their kids. Too bad the egg hunt had to end early. Maddox would be so disappointed. But the weather had changed so quickly.

She needed to get inside before the rain arrived. She didn't want to get drenched. Yet, as if glued to the pavement, she didn't move.

The sky turned a murky green. Her heart began to pound.

Abruptly, the wind stopped. The air stilled. And a weird, almost oppressive feeling hung in the atmosphere.

Shayla joined her on the sidewalk. "I'll see you tomorrow morn—" Looking past Kara, she frowned. "What's that on the mountain?" She pointed at the western range.

Turning, Kara's eyes widened. Out of the dark wall of clouds on the horizon, a thin, grayish funnel, lit by intermittent flashes of lightning, swirled and gyrated. In a sort of insane, macabre dance on the mountain. A dance of destruction and death.

And it was headed toward Truelove.

The tornado siren blared. She jolted. The piercing wail crescendoed. But she only had eyes for Maddox. Hands over his ears, the little boy sat down on the ground.

With the storm bearing down upon them, she raced

across the street and scooped him up in her arms. The child shook like a leaf. She was shaking like a leaf, too.

"Karwa," he cried, burrowing his face in her neck.

She patted his back. "I've got you, sweetie pie. I've got you."

"Take cover!" Mayor Watson shouted. "Everyone find shelter! Immediately!"

But where? None of the businesses were open. There was nowhere to go. In a matter of seconds, the cloudy afternoon sky transitioned into a malignant, midnight black.

People ran for their cars. She lost sight of Maggie, Wilda and the boys.

"There's no time to outrun it!" she yelled at the mayor. "Head them toward the café."

Nodding, he turned his attention to herding a frightened Mrs. Desmond and her yippy Chihuahua toward the safety of the café. Her baby son on her hip, Callie McAbee towed her daughter, Maisie, along. Kara motioned them toward the beckoning refuge of the restaurant.

The wind suddenly picked up again in speed and intensity. Debris flew. A falling tree branch whacked the mayor, knocking him off his feet. Shayla ran forward to help him and Mrs. Desmond.

With Maddox's legs in a stranglehold around her torso, Kara retraced her steps and encouraged everyone to keep moving forward. A sudden deluge of rain poured from the blackened sky. She shielded Maddox as best she could with her body.

Amber struggled to help a visibly trembling ErmaJean across the street. Slipping and sliding in the rain, Trudy dashed out to shepherd Lucy and Stella into the café.

His forehead glistening with a streak of blood, Mayor Watson manned the door. Keeping it open against the pulsing force of the wind as everyone scurried to safety. Lila held tightly on to Emma Cate. The last of the stragglers, AnnaBeth and Hunter, hustled IdaLee across the threshold.

Kara darted inside with Maddox and breathed a sigh of relief. Mayor Watson released the door. Shivering and dripping with rain, the storm-battered refugees huddled against the counter and every available space.

Her white hair blown out of its bun, IdaLee's blue-violet eyes scanned the interior. "Where's GeorgeAnne?" Her quavery voice rose. "Has anyone seen GeorgeAnne?"

"There she is." Maisie pointed out the window. "She's in the gazebo." She turned toward Callie. "Why doesn't she come inside with us, Mama?"

Everyone rushed toward the windows and stared at the lone figure hugging the railing on the steps of the gazebo.

"She's so afraid she can't move." ErmaJean put her hand to her throat. "GeorgeAnne's always been unusually terrified of thunderstorms."

The mayor heaved his not-inconsiderable bulk out of a booth. "I'll get her." But swaying, he fell against the seat, and he put a hand to his head.

Kara handed Maddox into ErmaJean's arms. "I'll go." And though she quavered at the prospect of facing the fury of the storm, she couldn't believe how calm and strong her voice sounded.

Maddox cried for his dad.

ErmaJean's face clouded. "Be careful out there, dear."

The overhead fluorescent lighting flickered and the electricity went out. A collective groan arose. Weblike crackling appeared in the sheet glass overlooking the square.

"Shayla. Trudy. Keep everyone back behind the counter." She swallowed. "Away from the windows."

Before she could talk herself out of it, she raced outside again. With each thunderous boom, her entire body quivered. She flinched with every sharp retort of lightning. The rain was falling almost horizontally. She tucked her head and ran the rest of the way.

Her iron-gray hair plastered to her head, the older woman stared at her. And in her wrinkled features, Kara beheld her own stark, mind-numbing fear. GeorgeAnne's mouth gaped but no sound emerged.

Kara dared not look behind her at the writhing thundercloud descending the mountain, jumping the river, speeding ever toward them. She yanked GeorgeAnne to her feet and such was her terror, the older woman murmured not a word of protest.

She tugged the matchmaker forward. Facing the full barrage of the wind, she felt as if their progress was minuscule. As if the air around them had become thick, soupy, quagmire-ish. Like something from a nightmare.

The woman tried to pull free. "Leave me."

"I won't." She refastened her hold on GeorgeAnne's arm. "Oh, God, help us," she whispered into the wind.

And GeorgeAnne seemed to regain some semblance of her old self. She added her strength to Kara's in battling forward across the square.

Mayor Watson waited for them at the entrance, holding the door. They staggered inside, skidding on the wet linoleum. The wind whipped the door shut behind them.

The café was dark, lit only by the faint illumination of cell phone screens. Huddled against the rear wall, people texted loved ones. IdaLee drew her fellow matchmaker behind the sheltering bulk of the counter. Maddox reached for Kara.

But over the roar of the wind, she detected a sound unlike anything she'd ever heard before. A strange, building roar. The howling grew ever more distinct. So much louder. So much closer. And her heart went cold.

"We have to get into the cooler now," she shouted. She threw open the porthole door. "Take Maddox, Miss Erma-Jean."

The wall of windows exploded.

Screams erupted as shards of glass flew in every direction. Scrambling to their feet, the small band rushed into the commercial kitchen. The mayor and the younger women half-shoved, half-guided the rest into the chilly darkness of the cooler.

When the last person disappeared into the cooler, she glanced back for one final look through the porthole at her beloved café.

The bell above the entrance jangled in a maniacal frenzy. There was a sucking, whistling sound. And then the wind ripped the door out of its steel frame. Silver napkin canisters rattled and crashed, sliding across the floor toward the opening as if pulled by a giant magnet.

And she knew if she didn't move now, she, too, might disappear into the black, gaping maelstrom.

Stumbling over her own feet, she threw herself inside the cooler. Wresting hold of the cooler door, she closed it as far as she could. But against the monstrous suction of the wind, how long could she hold it shut?

"Help me, God. Please, help me," she murmured.

Something, possibly one of the heavy iron skillets hanging above the range, collided against the other side of the door, slamming it the rest of the way shut.

Her back against the cold surface of the door, she sank to the floor. Wrenching himself free of ErmaJean, Maddox clawed his way to her. Except for the soft murmuring of prayers, the occupants of the makeshift tornado shelter were strangely quiet, even the children.

AnnaBeth shone the flashlight on her phone to provide

much-needed light. And several followed her example. For which Kara thanked God. Because despite everything else, darkness unrelieved by light was more than anyone should have to bear.

With nearly twenty people, there wasn't much room in the cooler. Some, like Amber, stood with their backs against the wire shelving. Others hunkered on the floor.

Outside the cooler, metal screeched. Objects pummeled the sides, shaking the walls. Mrs. Desmond's Chihuahua whimpered. The roar of the twister seemed to fill the very marrow of Kara's bones. It was like nothing she'd ever heard before or hoped to ever hear again.

She wanted to curl into a ball, but she did none of those things. Instead, she held on to Will's son. If necessary and with her last breath, she'd die to protect him.

Doing her best to hold it together, she thought of how terrified she'd been, watching her mother grow sicker and sicker. How helpless she'd felt, knowing inch by inch she was losing her. She also recalled how strong and brave and wonderful Mama G had been with her.

Kara whispered sweet words of comfort into Maddox's ear. Rubbing little circles onto his back, she told him everything would be okay. Because there was nothing scarier to a child than a scared grown-up.

Suddenly, the roaring eased. The cooler stopped shaking. The pummeling ceased. Cautiously, like turtles venturing from their shells, everyone looked at each other.

Emma Cate pulled at Lila's sleeve. "Is it over?"

The bride-to-be looked at her great-aunt IdaLee. "Maybe…"

Kara gulped. "I think so."

Cheers broke out among the children.

ErmaJean threw up her hands. "Thank you, Jesus."

GeorgeAnne locked gazes with Kara. "And Kara, too."

"Um…" Shifting, Amber grimaced. "I didn't want to mention it before, but I think my water broke."

Chapter Eleven

At the town limits, the first thing Will noticed was the absence of the Welcome sign. His stomach knotted, fearing how his beloved hometown might have fared during the tornado.

Speeding toward Truelove, his SUV clattered over the bridge spanning the river. The windshield wipers beat a steady cadence, but the rain looked to be slackening. The fire engine rolled into town behind him.

Yet, if he lived to be a hundred years old, he'd never forget the sight that met his eyes. In the aftermath of the tornado, devastation.

He blinked twice to clear his vision. To be sure what he beheld was actually real. But it was all too real. Wreaking havoc, the tornado had come and gone. Carving a path of destruction.

Many of the grand old trees encircling the square were gone. Torn from the ground, the trees lay like giant matchsticks across Main Street. Blocking access to the station and forcing the TFD to park on the edge of downtown.

Will got out of his vehicle, and the guys scrambled from the rig.

Luke grunted. "The gazebo's gone, Chief."

Jaw tight, he nodded. Not one board remained. Ripped off its foundation, only a large circular grassy spot bore evidence of where the gazebo once proudly stood.

Debris littered the streets. Misshapen hulks of metal that used to be cars had twisted like corkscrews around the trunks of the remaining trees. City Hall had lost its roof. Most of the building facades appeared battered. No telling what the interiors looked like.

Zach stood with his hands on his hips. "Good thing most businesses were closed today. Or who knows how many people could've been hurt."

For Zach's sake, he was relieved to see that the auto body shop was still standing. "We're going to fan out in pairs and check each building anyway to make sure no one is hurt or trapped inside. Use your radio to check in with Dispatch once you've cleared a building."

Several of the guys cut their eyes toward the still-intact firehouse. Department policy mandated that cell phones remained inside the station when fire crews responded to an incident. They were anxious to check on loved ones. But their duty to serve came first.

It was part of the job. Part of the firefighter life. What they'd signed on for. And their families knew it.

Checking on Pops would have to wait. Will's father and Tom Arledge were probably holed up at the Arledge farm trading fish tales instead of bait.

His transmitter crackled. Static erupted and then Nadine's voice. "… Hunt…" *Crackle. Crackle.* "… Café."

Will pressed the mic. "Repeat. I didn't copy. What is hunt—"

"The egg hunt, Chief." Luke scooped up a yellow plastic egg lying in the gutter. "The kids. This afternoon."

Static crackled from the transmitter.

Zach frowned. "But it would've been over ages ago, right?"

"Unless there was a rain delay." Will sucked in a breath. "And they took shelter at the diner."

He took off running toward the restaurant.

But on the sidewalk outside the Mason Jar, he skidded to a standstill. Shards of glass glittered on the pavement. The café looked like a bomb had gone off inside. The door was nowhere to be seen. The windows were smashed.

Surely, Maddox was somewhere else with ErmaJean. But Kara spent most afternoons here, baking for the next day. She could be in there and hurt. Or worse.

A cold terror gripped him. The kind of horror he believed he'd forever left behind when Maddox was released from the NICU. Moving forward, he stumbled. "Kara!" he shouted.

"Chief, wait!" Zach called after him. "Let me help."

"Stay back!" He threw up his hand. "I'm going in alone."

He knew he needed to assess structural damage before entering. But he didn't stop to think. He didn't care about anything other than finding her. He surged forward. Glass crunched under his boots.

And then the most beautiful sight he'd ever beheld— Kara, her hair disheveled and her clothes torn, staggered out onto the sidewalk.

Maddox's arms were tightly wrapped around her neck. "Daddy!"

Still in his turnout coat, Will reached for him. Maddox fell into his arms. "Kara?"

But she'd turned away. He wasn't sure if she'd even heard him. She stared at the wreck of the Mason Jar. The wreck of her dream.

To his amazement, people started pouring out of the

Mason Jar. A handful at first. Then a baker's dozen and more. Until the sidewalk was crowded with women and children.

Zach rushed forward when he spotted his great-aunt IdaLee. Lila and AnnaBeth stood beside the diminutive old woman. IdaLee had her arms around both their small children.

Bradley patched up Mayor Watson. Callie McAbee had her arm around Amber Green's shoulders. Shayla had Callie's little boy perched on her hip. Trudy held Callie's daughter, Maisie, by the hand.

A trained EMT before he landed the part-time job at the TFD, Luke came to Amber's assistance. Owing to her advanced labor, there was no way she'd make it over the mountain to the nearest hospital in time.

It became glaringly obvious Amber was a nurse. Even in the face of progressively intense contractions, she remained calm. She made the decision to deliver her baby at the nearby pediatrician's office.

He tasked one of the crew to venture on foot to fetch Ethan, Amber's husband.

ErmaJean held on to Lucy and Stella. "Check the workshop behind the house," she directed the firefighter. She gave the twins a big smile. "What an exciting day. You're going to be big sisters soon."

When Will looked around again, Kara was nowhere to be seen. He wished he'd had more time to make sure she was all right. But there were a thousand matters to be dealt with. A hundred questions to be answered.

He set up a temporary command center at the fire station until Bridger could return. Will needed to concentrate on search and rescue, but he wasn't sure what to do about Maddox. To his relief, Pops appeared and took Maddox home. Which Will was thankful to hear remained intact.

Word soon spread about the destruction. The tornado in its fickle fashion had wiped out some locations and left the adjacent structures untouched. People, who'd ridden out the storm safely, emerged from the surrounding neighborhoods to lend a hand. There were many gratitude-filled reunions as loved ones lost were found.

He kept a lookout for Kara, but she wasn't downtown. He figured she must have walked home. It was hard for him to see the damage the Jar had sustained. How much worse for her.

Over the next hour working alongside Bridger, a nagging concern for Kara continued to dog him.

Prickly as a pineapple and with an independent streak a mile wide, she wouldn't welcome his interference. As soon as he could safely turn operations over to his lieutenant, he'd track her down. If for nothing more than to satisfy his own aching need to reassure himself she was indeed okay.

Unable to bear the sad sight of the Mason Jar, Kara turned her back on the café. In a daze, she began walking away from the scene of the disaster. Heading toward her rental, it made her sick to think of all her money down the drain for renovations.

And she worried how long it would take the insurance check to come in. Hurrying down Main Street, she dodged the debris-littered sidewalks and turned into her neighborhood. Anxiety over how long the café would have to remain closed for repairs fretted the edges of her mind.

She slipped her hand into her skirt pocket. Her fingers touched cold metal. Taken aback, she stopped in front of IdaLee Moore's Victorian. She'd forgotten that she'd stuck the mini Eiffel Tower into her pocket. She still wasn't sure why, but she was glad she had. She had so little of her mom. Only memories.

Kara recalled how strong her mother had been in the face of her father's sudden death. How brave she'd been when they were evicted from their apartment. When they'd been forced to live out of their car. When her mother was diagnosed with cancer and faced impending death.

Raising her chin, Kara gave herself a good talking-to. She had her health. She and Mama G would rebuild the café. She might have lost Will and Maddox. But she had new friends. Her heart would heal. Eventually. *Right?*

She was so very thankful everyone on the square had survived the tornado. She'd survived so much already. She would survive this setback, as well.

And she also had a little creature in her life, waiting for her to give him his dinner. Possibly frightened by the storm. Probably scratching at the door and needing the comfort of his human. She could do with some tabby-style comfort herself.

Everything would be fine. She was a fighter and she'd rise from this latest challenge, as well.

Squaring her shoulders, she continued down the sidewalk to her rental. She was pleased to see IdaLee's house looked undisturbed. And also Lila's quaint, pale yellow bungalow next door. Rounding the corner to her street, she ground to a halt.

Wait. Her heart skipped a beat. *Her house.* Her stomach lurched. *Where was her house?*

In the capricious, random nature of tornados, the twister had hopscotched down Main Street, passed over IdaLee's street without harm, and apparently touched down once more on Kara's block. Ripping off the roof. Collapsing the walls. Scattering the contents of her life to the four winds. Stripping her house down to the foundation.

The details ran helter-skelter through her mind as she

raced toward what remained. "Soufflé!" she cried. "Soufflé!"

However, even as she searched, ploughing through detritus, lifting up broken shards of paneling, she knew. Nothing could've survived underneath the weight of the house. Not a human, much less a tiny cat.

But that didn't stop her from sifting through the rubble. Tears poured down her cheeks. Her fingernails tore. Her hands grimy, she swiped at her face, not caring about the dirt she left behind.

She didn't know why she continued. Only if nothing else, that she had to keep looking for Soufflé's broken little body. Although, what she'd do when she found him she didn't stop to consider.

What ran through her mind on a replaying loop was how much he needed her. She had to find him. She had to.

Kara sobbed. She raged. No one else might need her, or want her in this town. But Soufflé did. He loved her. Not many people had loved her. But Soufflé had.

"Soufflé!" she screamed. "Where are you? Can you hear me?"

This couldn't be happening. Not to her. Not again. Losing everyone and everything she'd ever cared about in one fell swoop.

"No. No. No."

Eventually, her strength, her frenzy, ran its course. She stumbled over a brick. She fell against a splintered two-by-four, scraping her arm and drawing blood. But she didn't care.

She did a slow turn, unable to take in or absorb the complete wreckage of her life. All at once, the hope that had always been such a hallmark of her personality deserted her. Including the optimism her mother had bequeathed to her in the face of homelessness, disease and death.

Without it—without hope—there was nothing. Nothing left to fight for. Nothing left to believe in. Nothing would ever get better for her.

Nothing.

"Where are you, God?" she rasped.

Her deepest, darkest fears had become reality. How had this happened to her? How had she found herself in this place again?

Swaying, her knees gave out on her.

Despite everything she'd done to outrun it. Despite Mama G. Despite culinary school. Despite her drive and hard work.

Kara sank to the ground.

She was homeless again. The ever-lurking bogeyman of her childhood had found her once more. She was still the same frightened, hungry child who'd lost her father, her home, soon to lose her mother. Her entire world. And this...

This was the last straw. Who could survive this? Not her. Not hit after unrelenting hit.

She'd never felt as alone, as heartsick or as lost in her life.

Zach appeared at his elbow. "Chief."

Coordinating the rescue efforts, Will looked up from the residential map of Truelove tacked to the wall of the fire station. No fatalities thus far. A few minor injuries.

Some of the orchards had suffered crop damage, but thankfully, no lives were lost. The church had escaped unscathed. Most of the property damage was minimal.

And everyone everywhere—courtesy of the Truelove grapevine—was talking about Kara's quick-thinking courage. She'd saved lives. She was a hero.

"My aunt IdaLee says you need to come." Zach clutched his helmet in his hands. "Right now."

IdaLee had been one of the people who rode out the tornado in the diner. He could've sworn he'd seen Lila and her fiancé take IdaLee home. Sam had rushed back from a job site near Asheville as soon as he heard the report on the radio.

"Is Miss IdaLee having some sort of delayed reaction?"

The men were slowly working their way in concentric circles through the surrounding neighborhoods, going door-to-door assessing the damage and making sure everyone was okay. He'd sent Zach and some of the other volunteers to the older, historic neighborhood where IdaLee lived.

"It's Kara, sir. Aunt IdaLee says you need to come quick."

Will's heart leaped into his throat. "What's wrong with Kara?"

"Her house is gone, Chief. Destroyed. Everything inside, too." Zach looked at the floor. "And she can't find her cat. She's been searching the block for hours."

"Oh, no." Poor Soufflé. "Kara must be devastated."

"AnnaBeth and Mrs. Desmond down the block have been trying to get her to come inside Aunt IdaLee's house. But she won't leave until she finds her cat." Zach swallowed. "Yet, if she did locate the little guy, I hate to think what she'd actually find…"

He locked eyes with the young man. "That mustn't be allowed to happen."

Zach nodded.

"Tell Miss IdaLee I'm on my way."

Until the streets were cleared, it would be quicker to walk versus driving over in his vehicle. The nagging concern he'd felt earlier had turned into a raging, frantic desperation to reach her.

He jogged past the square and the diner. Reaching the neighborhood, he spotted IdaLee on her porch, her cell pressed to her ear. He practically ran the last two blocks. Out of breath, his chest heaving, he ground to a stop beside the small band of onlookers.

Lila was crying. Sam had his arm around her. Jonas Stone cradled his hat in his hands, looking as helpless as all of them felt.

Kara had always been petite, but until this moment he'd never seen how fragile the feisty chef truly was. Nor how precious she was to him.

"Please, Kara, honey..." Mrs. Desmond cajoled. "Let's get you a nice strong cup of tea. With lots of sugar."

It may have been the first time he'd ever seen the portly older woman without her Chihuahua.

He took a step inside the circle of debris.

Poking at a pile of rubble, Kara's head shot up. "No. Stop."

He was taken aback by the vehemence in her voice. Dried tears stained her cheeks. His heart twisted. Her elbow was scraped and bleeding. Torn and dirty, her skirt was probably past salvaging.

AnnaBeth gave him an anguished look. "She's afraid someone might step on Soufflé and hurt him."

He glanced at the sky. It would be dark soon. The light was slowly beginning to fade. She couldn't stay out here all night.

"Kara, please... Talk to me..."

"I can't." Head bent once more, she returned to her fruitless search. "Got to find Soufflé. He doesn't like the dark."

"Let me help you find the tabby." He stretched out his hand. "Please, darlin'. You don't have to do this alone."

She raised her gaze. "But I am alone."

And something—perhaps the final wall he'd erected around his heart—shattered inside him.

"I have to find Soufflé, Will." She tilted her head. "When Maddox finds out that Soufflé is—" her voice caught "—is missing, he'll be so upset."

"Don't worry, Kara. I'll make sure he understands. It'll be okay."

She gave him a faint, sad smile that broke his heart. "People always say that, but it isn't true, you know. I thought maybe just this once…" She looked beyond him toward town. "That perhaps here it would be. But it isn't. It never is." She bit her lip. "Not for me."

"It's too dark to look anymore, Kara. But I promise I'll be out here at first light searching for your cat."

She studied him. "I never went looking for a pet. But the stray found me. You had it right all along about not opening your heart. Not trusting. Not loving. I wish…" She sighed. "It doesn't matter what I wish."

He blinked back the moisture dotting his eyes. He wasn't right about love. Not about so many things, especially when it came to Kara.

A silver Mercedes pulled up to the corner. Glorieta Ferguson got out of the car. Gray silk scarf fluttering behind her, she hurried over. "I was already headed back to Truelove when I heard the news bulletin."

Lila drew her aside and filled her in on what was happening.

The barbecue queen gave him a steely mama bear look. "I can't think when I've been as disappointed in someone as I have in you, young man."

"Not nearly as disappointed as I am in myself right now, Miss Glorieta. How did you know about…?"

Her plum-lined lips thinned. "Never doubt an honorary matchmaker. Our network is everywhere."

Aka Pops.

"Now, step aside." She shouldered past Will, stopping at the perimeter of the debris field. "Kara." Her voice became brisk. "I'm going to need you to come with me now, sweet child. Right this minute."

Kara turned. "Mama G? What're you doing here?"

Glorieta held out her hand. "It's time to go, sugar. Time to come home."

Kara's delicate shoulders drooped. "I don't have a home, Mama G. Why does this keep happening to me?"

Why does what keep happening to her? Will felt like he was missing something. Something vital he didn't understand about Kara.

Had she lived through a tornado before? Is that why she'd known what to do earlier for the people caught in the storm at the square?

Glorieta's chin wobbled, but her tone held firm. "Everyone is concerned about you. You're scaring us, honey."

Her forehead puckering, for the first time Kara seemed to notice the others standing nearby. "I didn't mean to worry anyone."

"I know you didn't." Glorieta opened her palm. "Take my hand, sugar pie. Please."

She took a step toward her foster mom. And another.

"Why does everyone always leave me?" Her eyes cut to Will, spearing his heart. "Ev-everyone." Her voice hitched.

"God doesn't, Kara." Glorieta grabbed her hand, pulling her closer, away from the destruction. "Not ever."

AnnaBeth released a gust of breath. The relief among the rest was palpable. Lila sagged against Sam.

Shock setting in, Kara quivered like a beech leaf in a winter gale. Taking off his TFD jacket, Will slipped it around her shoulders. What he really wanted to do was to take her in his arms, but he'd given up the right to do that.

Mrs. Desmond moved to stand on Kara's other side. "I live around the corner, Miss Glorieta. And I have so many empty rooms since my children flew the nest. Perhaps you two would take supper with me this evening?"

Glorieta's cheeks lifted. "I thank you kindly for the invitation." Lines fanned out from the corners of her dark eyes. "My Kara and I would be most pleased to accept."

The two women continued to converse as they led Kara slowly down the block. He watched them walk away and he so wanted to make everything better for her. But even if it had been within his power, his comfort was the last thing on earth she would have welcomed.

A few hours later he left the station in the capable hands of Bradley. He needed to check on his father and son. At the flash of his headlights turning into the driveway, Maddox appeared, waiting for him inside the storm door.

Wearing his pint-size firefighter hat, his little boy waved. And his heart lifted. No day was ever so bad his son couldn't brighten it.

Maddox had the door open for him before he was halfway up the steps.

"I can't stay long." He gathered Maddox into his arms and kissed his head. "Just wanted to check on you two."

Kara had most probably saved his child's life today. Saved him again.

Wiping his hands on a dish towel slung over his shoulder, Pops turned from the stove. "I kept your dinner warm."

"I don't really—"

"Running on fumes doesn't do anybody any good." Pops plopped a helping of the stovetop concoction on a plate. "You need to refuel."

"Any word from across the street about Amber and her baby?"

Pops emptied the dishwasher. "ErmaJean called just before you arrived. Mother and son are doing well."

He heaved a sigh of relief. "Finally, some good news out of this day."

Maddox hovered at his elbow while Will shoveled food into his mouth. "When can I see Karwa, Daddy?"

He winced. Pops gave him a look like *yeah, Dad, explain your way out of this one*.

"Can I go feed Soufflé tomorrow?"

He put down his fork. "I need to tell you something, son. And you're going to have to be very, very brave."

Pops pulled out a chair at the table and sat down. "What's happened?"

Will took Maddox into his lap and explained how the tornado had destroyed Kara's little house.

Pops shook his head. "I'm sorry to hear that. And with the café out of commission, too, she must be feeling overwhelmed."

Maddox's brows bunched. "Miss Karwa and Soufflé can stay at our house. It's better when she's here anyway."

It *was* better when Kara was with them. Unfortunately, he'd come to that realization too late for it to matter. And he still hadn't told his son the worst part—that thanks to Will's hardheaded stupidity he'd lost Kara from their lives forever.

His son adored Soufflé. Maddox would be devastated about the cat.

Will took a deep breath. "When I told you about Kara's house, Maddox..."

"Dat de big wind blew ev-wee-ding," Maddox opened his arms to illustrate. "Far, far away."

"Everything inside the house is gone, son."

Catching on, Pops groaned. "Oh, no."

"Kara looked and looked, Maddox, but Soufflé is gone, too."

Maddox blinked slowly several times until realization dawned in his chocolate-brown eyes. "No, Daddy." He shook his head.

Will hugged his son to his chest. "I'm so, so sorry, Maddox."

He stayed longer than he intended, but he needed to be there for his son. Gazing down at his sleeping child, he tucked the covers around his precious boy. The truth about losing Kara sat heavy on his chest. But that disclosure would have to wait a while longer.

Because neither his nor Maddox's heart could take any more sadness tonight.

Chapter Twelve

Unfortunately, the numbness that shrouded Kara after the loss of her cat didn't last. She spent the rest of the long, long night in one of Mrs. Desmond's elegant guest rooms in clothes borrowed from Lila. Sobbing her heart out. Cradled in Mama G's enveloping embrace.

When she awoke the next morning, daylight streamed through the lace curtains. She awoke groggy and disoriented, unsure of where she was at first. Then yesterday's events slammed into her consciousness, and she moaned.

Glorieta sprang up out of the blue armchair next to the bed. "Sugar?"

"I—I must've fallen asleep."

Her foster mom grasped her hand on top of the bedcovers. "In the wee hours of the night."

Kara's throat felt hoarse from her tears. The usually immaculate woman looked disheveled. Her gray silk pantsuit rumpled.

She struggled to sit upright on the bed. "You didn't spend the night in that chair, did you?"

It seemed to Kara that new wrinkles dotted the creases around Glorieta's eyes. Mama G sank down onto the mattress beside her.

"And what if I did?" The barbecue queen tossed her head. "Aren't I old enough to decide when and where I want to go to bed, or if at all?" She wagged her finger. "If my girl is hurting, I'm hurting, too."

"The best day's work I ever did was sneak into your kitchen."

Glorieta's mouth quirked. "And the best day's work I ever did was bring you home with me." Her smile dimmed. "Rick called and told me what happened between you and Will. That's why I was already on my way when the storm hit Truelove."

Kara took a deep, shuddering breath. "I love Will, but he didn't see a future with me."

"He wouldn't allow himself to. And before you go blaming yourself, Will MacKenzie's got unresolved issues that have nothing to do with you." Glorieta's jaw tightened. "I could just shake a knot in that fire chief, and Rick would probably help me."

Kara straightened. "What's done is done. Don't go and make things worse."

Although, she wasn't sure how the situation could get much worse. She'd lost her livelihood and Mama G's investment, too. She'd lost her home. And sweet Soufflé.

"Hmm…"

She didn't like the look in Glorieta's eyes. She'd seen the tenderhearted-to-a-fault lady once before go full bore on Terence's college sweetheart, who'd done him wrong. It was a tongue-lashing, Kara would hazard a guess, that young miss had never forgotten.

"Mama G…"

Glorieta fluttered her hand. "And don't you think Cedrick and Terence won't have something to say about all this, too."

Kara let her head fall back on the pillow. "Must we

get the boys involved?" But the reminder that she wasn't really alone did her heart a world of good. As no doubt, Mama G intended.

Her back straight and her shoulders squared, Glorieta sat prim and proper as a schoolmarm. But there was a twinkle in her gaze.

Kara laughed at the picture Mama G painted of an avenging Cedrick and Terence. Their mother was definitely a force of nature. But the boys, former ACC offensive linemen turned corporate execs, were mild as cinnamon toast. And about as sweet.

Glorieta chuckled. "Well, now that we've got the gloomies off your pretty face, let's get down to business. How do you want to handle where we go from here?"

Cut to the chase, no-nonsense, bottom-line Mama G. One of the things she most admired and loved about her foster mom. She rejoiced over her children's triumphs and grieved each of their setbacks. But no one was allowed to wallow. Not for long.

Exactly what Kara needed to hear.

"The restaurant—"

Glorieta waved her hand. "This is why we have insurance."

"Every day closed for repair is another day's profits lost." She pleated the edge of the sheet with her fingers. "We were barely breaking even."

"We'll make it work." Never say die, Glorieta thumped the mattress. "I've got faith in your success."

"That's just it. I'm not sure I do anymore. At least not in Truelove." Kara looked at her, a long, steady moment. "It's not just the café."

Glorieta squeezed her hand. "Tell me what you're thinking. How you're feeling."

"Maybe the tornado was a sign I don't belong here."

Her foster mom bristled. "I've told you like I've told all my children. You belong where you say you belong."

If only life were that simple.

"When Will broke things off, my plan was to continue at the Mason Jar. Pour myself into cooking. Make a life, even if that life didn't include him and Maddox. But…"

Glorieta frowned. "You want to throw in the towel? That doesn't sound like my Kara."

"Your Kara never had her heart wrung out like a wet dishrag before," she rasped.

"Oh, honey."

"And now that Soufflé is…" She worked hard to keep the wobble out of her voice. "Now that Soufflé isn't around anymore, I have to wonder what's the point in fighting the inevitable. The town doesn't want me here. They don't like my food. They don't like me. Maybe it isn't God's will that I stay."

"You have more supporters than detractors. And more friends than you realize." Glorieta pointed to Kara's phone on the bedside table. "You slept through tons of messages. People thanking you for saving their lives. And their children. Their grandchildren. And all of them wanting to know how you're doing."

"Not so well, Mama G…" she whispered.

"That's how you feel now, but you won't feel that way forever." Glorieta pursed her lips. "Trust me, I've lived long enough to see the truth of that many times over."

"I know how you can't abide a quitter." Her eyes watered. "I wanted so much not to let you down."

Glorieta took both of her hands. "If you decide you want to walk away from this venture, you won't be letting me down. But in the space of seventy-two hours, you've suffered multiple losses. You need time to grieve and process each one. I don't think you should make any life-altering decision until you've taken this to the Lord and sought His wisdom."

"You're right." Kara gave her a small smile. "As usual. But don't let it go to your head."

Glorieta cupped her cheek. "There's my girl. I knew she was still in there. You've had your feet knocked out from under you, but when you're ready, you'll stand straight and strong again and I'll be standing there with you."

"I thought the saying was 'straight and tall'?"

"You know I can't abide a lie." Glorieta batted her lashes. "And, sugar pie, you ain't never gonna be tall."

Laughing, Kara fell over on the bed.

Glorieta got off the mattress. "I think I should check on the café. Take some photos and then contact our insurance agent."

She threw back the covers. "Would you?"

"Be glad to. And you mind what I said yesterday about God never leaving or forsaking you, either."

She swung her legs over the side of the bed and planted her feet firmly on the carpet. "I love you, Mama G."

Glorieta blew her a kiss. "I love you, too." Her foster mom closed the bedroom door behind her.

Kara picked up the tiny Eiffel Tower she'd carefully placed there last night before dissolving into tears. A visual reminder of God's continuing faithfulness.

God had been there for her when her father died. He'd been there protecting her and her mom when they had to live in their vehicle. He'd secured a place for them at the family homeless shelter. And put Mama G into her life after her mother's death.

Through it all, she'd never been alone. With eyes of renewed faith, she saw it clearly as if for the first time. God's hand had been on her life from the beginning. His hand would be on her now and forever.

She would think, pray and listen for the Lord's counsel as to her next step. He would sustain her through all of life's trials. He would be there for her every step of the way. Whether in Truelove or in some yet unknown destination.

God had gifted her to give love to others through food. And if not in Truelove, He would direct her path to where He needed her the most.

Setting the small object on the bedside table again, she shuffled into the en-suite bathroom to shower and get dressed. And if she did leave Truelove, there were a lot of issues that would have to be resolved before she left the Jar behind.

Not the least of which would be helping Leo, Shayla and Trudy find new employment. The property would need to be repaired and listed for sale with a Realtor. And no matter where she found herself, she'd make sure she did right by Lila and Sam's wedding reception.

But God would make all things come together for her in the end. And in faith, she chose to hang on to that truth.

As for her heart?

Bleakly, she stared at her reflection in the bathroom mirror. Her heart would hurt for a long, long time to come.

Somehow, Will managed to get several hours of sleep in his office at the firehouse, but at first light the weekend shift came on to relieve the weekday crew. And for the next few hours, he combed through the rubble at Kara's house.

"You and I need to talk."

He jolted. Glorieta stood on the edge of the debris field. But he'd been so intent on his search he hadn't heard her approach. This was exactly what he didn't need—but probably deserved—getting chewed out by Kara's foster mom.

Most likely inevitable, though. Maybe it was best to get it over with now. The sun shone out of a breezy blue sky.

No clouds in sight. He'd lost track of time. By the angle of the sunlight, it must already be about midmorning.

He blew out a breath. "How did you know I was here?"

"I saw you when I was getting ready to head to the café." She adjusted the purple silk scarf around her throat. "What are you doing?"

He shifted a board. "I figured Kara would be out here later to gather whatever remained of her personal belongings." He shoved aside a chunk of concrete that might have been a porch step. "I wanted to make sure she didn't accidentally stumble across Soufflé."

Using the jagged remnants of a piece of rebar, he continued to poke, prod and look under the wreckage. Several beats of silence ticked by.

"That's very…"

He glanced up at the older woman again.

"Compassionate? Considerate? A kind gesture?" She folded her arms. "Especially from a man who told my Kara he didn't-shouldn't-wouldn't love her and then walked away. Perhaps you could explain that to me, son."

Will kept his gaze trained on the scattered wreckage of what had been Kara's kitchen. "It's complicated, Miss Glorieta."

He spotted a fragment of one of Kara's rooster-red mixing bowls. Images flooded his mind of being with her and Maddox in this very room. The fun, the laughter, the joy.

Gone forever, just like this little house where for a short instant in time he'd known such happiness. A happiness some part of him had known couldn't last.

Kara's foster mom moved to stand beside him. "I've always found life is generally about as complicated as we make it." She propped her hands on her ample hips. "Do you love my girl, Will?"

Unable to face her, he became extremely busy excavating the rubbish in the corner.

"Your care for her feelings over that little cat tells me that you do."

He swung around. "Yes, I love Kara."

It was a relief in finally being able to say the words out loud.

His shoulders drooped. "But none of that matters. I learned my lesson with Liz. It's better I end things now before..." He pinched his lips together.

"Before what?" Her expression cleared. "Oh, Will. You felt you needed to walk away before Kara walked away from you."

"I lost my job. Maddox and I have to relocate. Kara's life is here with the Mason Jar." He clenched his jaw. "There was no future for us."

"Did it ever occur to you to ask Kara what she wanted?"

"She's devoted her life to making this dream a reality." He shook his head. "I would never ask her to give that up."

"What makes you assume she couldn't have both?"

"But the Jar—"

"If push had come to shove between you and the restaurant, there would've been no contest." Glorieta looked down the length of her nose at him. A considerable feat considering he topped the woman by half a foot. "You and Maddox were the dream. The restaurant merely the means to an end."

He frowned. "I don't understand."

"That's because you haven't been listening." She sniffed. "A common enough problem among your gender. That, and underestimating mine." Her eyes flashed. "What was the first thing I told you about Kara?"

He cast his mind back. "That Kara gives her love by feeding people?"

Glorieta rolled her eyes. "Got it in one, ladies and gentlemen." She ticked off on her fingers. "So she made it her business to feed first this town, then Maddox, your dad, you, a stray cat… Which is exactly why she feels she has no choice but to abandon the town that won't accept her."

"Wait. What?" He widened his stance. "She's leaving Truelove? She can't do that."

"She doesn't believe there's anything left for her here." Glorieta leveled her gaze at him. "Is she right?"

"I love her, Miss Glorieta. Maddox does, too." He threw the rebar down. It landed with a clang. "I can't imagine anything more wonderful than making a life, a family, a home, with her but—"

"No buts." The barbecue queen waved his words away with her hand. "That's all I needed to know before I told you the rest. Kara explained how we first came to meet each other?"

He wasn't sure where she was going with this, but he nodded. "Her mom was sick. She wandered into the kitchen of a homeless shelter where a volunteer in a funny hat was whipping up dinner." He blinked rapidly. "It guts me to think how little, how scared, how hungry she must've been."

"I took one look at that child and knew—just knew—that somehow the Lord had given me her to be the daughter I always wanted." Glorieta's lips trembled. "I'm glad she shared that with you. She doesn't tell many people the whole story. And I'm not sure even now she truly grasps the depth of what it reveals of her."

"Love equals food to Kara."

"No, my dearest William." Glorieta squeezed his arm. "Love equals home. She smelled the food and she was hungry. But the food reminded her of happier times. The smells made her hungry for home. And she's been trying to recreate home for herself ever since."

He pinched the bridge of his nose and closed his eyes. "In Truelove. At the Mason Jar. This small rental house. With Soufflé."

With sudden clarity, he understood why she'd been so shattered yesterday. Desperately searching for the cat, her dreams in ruins all around her. Amid the desolation of her home.

"Most of all, she longed with all of her being to make a home with you and Maddox." Glorieta touched his arm. "You don't need to be afraid of Kara ever becoming like your ex-wife. It's simply not in her. But perhaps it isn't Kara you distrust, but yourself."

"I failed Liz. And because of my failure, Maddox lost his mother. I couldn't bear to fail Kara or let Maddox down again."

"You're not the only one who knows a little something about folks walking away." Glorieta took his hand into her warm, calloused palm. "I understand all too well the scars, the bitterness and the wreckage it leaves behind in your heart."

He took a ragged breath.

"Don't think I haven't agonized over what my boys may have suffered because of the failure of my marriage. But God is bigger than my issues or their father's. So much bigger than our failures. God loves me. He loves my boys. He loved a scared little girl in a homeless shelter."

She gripped his hand so hard he winced. "He loves you, dear Will, and your precious child. God will never walk away. He'll never leave nor forsake you. And with God on your side, you've already won."

"I don't know what to do, Miss Glorieta. I don't know

how to fix me." He pounded his fist on his chest. "I don't know how to fix what's broken inside me."

"Of course you don't." Her chin came up. "Because you're not God."

His chest heaved.

"Best thing you, or any of us, can do is to give the hurt, the anger, the doubts, the fear and the bitterness over to Him." She cocked her head. "'Cause it's not like He doesn't know about it already."

Will had to laugh, despite himself.

"There is a balm in Gilead." She shook her finger at him. "Forgive Liz. Forgive yourself. And let God pour over your ashes the healing oil of gladness." She smiled.

He planted a quick kiss on her cheek. "Thank you, Miss Glorieta, for caring enough to set me straight."

"Don't you know I'm a sucker for a handsome man with manners?" She gave him a wink. "Speaking of handsome, charming men, maybe I'll stop by to see your dad on my way to the Jar."

"Pops would love that." He swallowed past the lump in his throat. "Have I told you how happy I am that you and Pops are friends?"

The barbecue queen's lips curved. "While you're having your come-to-Jesus moment, don't forget to ponder what you can do to convince Kara not to leave Truelove. When that girl sets her mind to something, she can be so stubborn."

"Wonder where she gets that from."

Glorieta laughed so hard, tears leaked out of her eyes. "This is why I took one look at you, Will MacKenzie, and knew right then and there you two were perfect for each other." Still chuckling, she gave him a wave and headed back toward Mrs. Desmond's.

For the next hour he sat down on the rough, broken step

and undisturbed, he cried out to God. After a while, his mind quieted. His heart settled. Peace flooded his being.

There was only the scratching of a robin underneath a bush. And the gentle whisper of the wind sloughing through the trees.

But what could he do to get Kara to change her mind about leaving town? Truelove needed her a whole lot more than she needed them.

He raked his hand over his head. Truth was, he needed Kara in his life a lot more than she could ever possibly need him.

"I messed up bad with her, God," he whispered to the wind. "Let my fears and insecurities overshadow what I felt in my heart for her."

Where do I go from here? Help me, Lord. Show me what to do to win back her heart.

His gaze wandered over the shambles around him. So far he'd managed to find the mangled metal of what was left of Soufflé's crate, but nothing else. Maybe Maddox had it right. The wind had blown the poor, defenseless creature far, far away.

Slowly, an idea took root inside him. Perhaps it wouldn't change her decision, but it might help her to see how many people in Truelove did care about her and her restaurant.

He'd need assistance. A lot of assistance. Taking out his phone, he put in a call to ErmaJean. She answered on the first ring.

Skipping pleasantries about her new great-grandson, he quickly gave her the lowdown on the latest crisis to befall Truelove—losing Kara—and outlined his plan to get her to stay.

"I'll alert Ethan to text the menfolk, and I'll call Ida-Lee. We'll message every contact on our phones," Erma-

Jean promised. "Never fear, dear heart. Truelove is here for you."

He could almost envision the plump older lady fist-pumping the air.

Next stop—the hardware store to tackle GeorgeAnne. He grimaced. But anything for Kara.

Because when it came to rallying the town and marshaling the troops, there was nothing for it but to get the matchmakers involved.

Will would call in a few favors of his own, too. Enlist AnnaBeth and Lila. But he was running out of time. And the clock was ticking.

He had a feeling that if he didn't stop Kara from leaving Truelove, there would be no second chances. He would lose her forever.

Chapter Thirteen

The rest of the day proved completely frustrating for Kara.

She'd accomplished absolutely nothing on her Things That Must Be Done list. No matter how hard she tried, it was like she came up against a brick wall.

Lunchtime came and went. Not that she had an appetite. And what was even scarier, she'd lost all desire to create food. She picked at the chicken salad on a croissant Mrs. Desmond had left for her.

The chicken salad and croissant that was bought yesterday morning at the Mason Jar by her kind hostess before Kara's world blew to smithereens.

She called to congratulate Amber, resting at home with her newborn son. "I'm sure Lucy and Stella are over the moon in love with their baby brother. How are you feeling?"

"Uh, great. Yeah. They're happy. Sorry to cut this short, but I'm going to have to get off the phone now."

"Sure. I under—" *Click.*

Kara tried not to allow her feelings to be overly hurt at Amber's unseemly haste to get off the phone. She dialed her short-order cook next.

Leo answered, but as soon as she identified herself he yelped something in Spanish and hung up on her.

She stared at the cell in her hand with disbelief. And so it went. Her phone calls to say goodbye went unanswered. All afternoon she left messages, which all went unreturned.

AnnaBeth. Lila. Callie and Maggie. Shayla and Trudy were unavailable, too. Even Mrs. Desmond and her Chihuahua had made themselves scarce.

Where was everyone? Maybe they were involved in picking up the pieces of their own storm-tossed lives. Yards to be raked. Houses to be repaired. Insurance adjustors to contact.

Feeling stonewalled, she flopped across the bed.

Or perhaps with the Mason Jar gone, she'd outlived her usefulness to Truelove. And those she'd believed were friends for life were actually no more than friends for this particular, mountain-winding curve in the road.

She pinched the bridge of her nose.

This is what came from putting yourself out there for people to stomp all over your heart. Sunny, optimistic Kara needed a reality check. This was real life. This was her life. Better get used to it.

Will texted her three times. Which she promptly ignored, then deleted. Because at some point, Defeated Kara had given way to Scrappy Kara.

Midafternoon, Glorieta came back from the café with the photos she'd taken. "Minimal damage." Her foster mom swiped through the pictures on her cell. "Windows. Entrance door. Upholstery. But otherwise, the damage is cosmetic."

Kara pursed her lips. "There are gouges in the dining room walls. The paint job is ruined."

"But the equipment is undamaged. The kitchen area,

albeit windblown, is easily set to rights." Glorieta hitched her eyebrow. "Where there's a will, there's a way."

She grimaced. "No will here."

"Little *w* or big *W*?"

Kara glowered. "Both."

Smoothing the crease in her jeans, Glorieta stood up from Mrs. Desmond's green brocade couch. "I see."

And she got that look in her eye Kara had come to recognize warned that Glorieta was about to say something she'd rather not hear.

"Tomorrow's a-coming, Kara Lynn."

"Yes, ma'am. Easter Sunday. I know."

Glorieta moistened her lips. "Will was coming in as I was leaving. You two should talk."

"I think we've said about all there is to say to each other."

"Aren't you the least curious as to why he's at the café?"

"Nope. I'm not."

That wasn't true, but she quickly buried any yearning to see Will under a heavy layer of "fool me once, shame on you, fool me twice…"

"I'm going to tell you anyway."

Which Kara had known she would.

Glorieta gave her an imperious look. "He was assessing the electrical panel to make certain nothing had short-circuited and which might present a future fire hazard."

She sniffed. *Good for him.*

"He said he needed to talk to you."

Kara recalled the three texts she'd erased. "I'm not going down there. I don't want to talk to him."

"So you're never going to set foot inside the café again?"

Kara jutted her jaw. "Not if I can help it."

"What about your cooking journals?"

How could she have forgotten those? "Couldn't you bring them to me the next time you go downtown?"

"I could." Glorieta grabbed her purse. "But I won't."

Her eyes widened. "What? Why? Wait. You're leaving again?"

"You want your journals, you'll have to get them yourself, missy." Glorieta touched a hand to her close-cropped gray curls. "And yes, I'm headed out again. I have a date with a retired fire chief and his adorable grandson. There was talk of ice cream, I believe."

Her foster mom disappeared out the front door, and Kara threw a couch cushion onto the Persian rug. Pacing the floor, she was still fuming when the doorbell rang fifteen minutes later.

She peeked around the hallway toward the front door. Had Glorieta changed her mind and come back for her? She longed to cuddle Maddox with an intensity that made her ache inside.

Crossing the distance, she glanced quickly through the glass sidelight at the lengthening lavender shadows gathering across the green lawn before yanking open the door.

"Oh." She stepped back a fraction. "I didn't realize it was you."

GeorgeAnne's wrinkled mouth tightened. "And if you had, you wouldn't have answered the door."

She flushed.

"I wouldn't blame you if you shut the door in my face right this minute." GeorgeAnne's bony hand gripped her car keys. "But if you'd give me a chance, I'd like to make amends. To apologize for being such a...such a..."

"Glass of curdled milk? Rotten egg? Halibut gone bad?"

What passed for a smile with GeorgeAnne lightened her features. "That's what I like about you, Kara Lockwood. You've been a worthy opponent. Always such a kick in the pants to those who are overdue for it. Who've gotten a little too big for their britches. Reminds me of me."

For the love of quiche, please not that.

"Maggie and her boys corralled me into giving that galette thing of yours a try."

"I'm—"

"And by corralled, I mean that literally. Austin and Logan talked me into playing cowboys, then steered and roped me to a kitchen chair."

She put her hand over her mouth. "They tied you up?"

"Maggie wouldn't release me until I took a bite." GeorgeAnne scrunched up her face. "It wasn't half-bad. I had more than one bite, actually."

High praise from the acerbic leader of the Double Name Club.

GeorgeAnne pushed her glasses farther up her nose. "I can see where it should have its rightful place on the Mason Jar menu."

"Thank you… I think."

Quite a concession, considering it was *Kara's* menu, not GeorgeAnne's. But a moot point. Somehow, like the rest of Truelove, GeorgeAnne's highhanded ways had grown on her.

Kind of like kudzu.

"Not only did you save my life—"

"Miss GeorgeAnne…" She fidgeted.

GeorgeAnne held up her palm. "Not only did you save my life, but you're a valuable member of Truelove. The Mason Jar has always been the community's center, but you, Kara dear, have become its heartbeat."

Her eyes stung. "Thank you for saying that, Miss GeorgeAnne. It means more than you'll ever know."

"I wanted to stop by to apologize for what Walter assures me has been abominable behavior, unbecoming to a woman of my influence."

Kara straightened. "Walter's back in Truelove?"

"He's waiting in the car for me." The smile that flitted across GeorgeAnne's features was just this side of coy. "Once he heard about the tornado, he wanted to make sure I wasn't hurt."

"I'm glad."

GeorgeAnne peered at her. "I can see that you truly are. You really are the most extraordinary person. How blessed Chief MacKenzie will be to call you his wife."

Her heart twisted. "We're not together anymore, Miss GeorgeAnne."

"But I'm on the case now." The woman lifted her index finger. "As ErmaJean just this morning pointed out to me, I've neglected my greater calling as a matchmaker. An error I mean to rectify. Immediately."

Kara believed it best not to respond to that so she said nothing. Will didn't love her. There was no fixing that. And she didn't want anyone else.

"I also wanted to thank you for gracing us with your culinary skills." GeorgeAnne's glacier-blue eyes twinkled. "I hear that crème brûlée of yours isn't anything to sneeze at."

"Thank you for coming by, Miss GeorgeAnne."

And she meant it. Kara felt lighter. She'd always aimed to live in harmony with everyone. The conflict with the woman had weighed heavily on her.

GeorgeAnne tilted her head. "Seeing as you and I are so much alike…"

Dear Jesus, say it isn't so.

"I have one last piece of unsolicited advice."

That would be the day.

"I drove past the Mason Jar Café on my way here…" GeorgeAnne gave her a significant look.

And she realized it was the first time the older woman had called her restaurant by its new name. A token of respect. She smiled back.

"I do believe you might want to stop by and see for yourself what the fire chief tore out of your kitchen. A bunch of books were on top of the pile."

"What?" she shrieked. "How dare he? Who does he think he is?"

Her precious cooking journals. Was nothing sacred? The man had the taste buds of a barbarian, which she'd tried her utmost to cultivate and educate. But obviously, some things were beyond the ability of a mortal woman.

GeorgeAnne chuckled, grating across Kara's taut nerves like a metal shish-kebab skewer across a too-hot griddle. "I think my work here is done." She turned on her heel and headed to her truck, parked at the curb.

An older gentleman, silver-haired and eminently distinguished, waved, but Kara was too undone to return the courtesy.

She grabbed Mrs. Desmond's spare key. During the tornado, Kara's car had been parked behind the restaurant, and thus had escaped damage. AnnaBeth's husband, Jonas, had thoughtfully returned her car last night. But Kara didn't bother taking her vehicle the few short blocks between Mrs. Desmond's and downtown.

Break her heart if he must. But if William Lane Mac-Kenzie had laid a finger on her journals… If he thought he could erase her from this town, his heart, like yesterday's blue plate special…

He better think again.

She stomped down the block, carried along by a fine head of steam, which had only just begun to build. The fire chief might believe he'd seen his fair share of amazing blazes, but she was coming to set him straight. And when she got through with him… She gnashed her teeth.

Nobody, but nobody, did blaze better than a chef.

When he finished reading the text from GeorgeAnne, Will pocketed his phone. "We don't have much time before Kara arrives."

AnnaBeth placed the last sprig of wildflowers in the glass Mason jar. "The paint on the walls may still be a bit tacky to the touch, but otherwise everyone is nearly finished."

They stood in the middle of the dining area. At the moment it was organized chaos. But administration was his strong suit. Evaluating a situation, developing a plan for action and deploying his crew to where most needed to make a difference.

He could have done none of this, though, without Anna-Beth's design guidance. Will took a quick survey of all they'd accomplished in such a short time. "I think we might actually pull this off."

AnnaBeth distributed the Mason jars filled with wildflowers to each of the tables. "O ye of little faith. How could you have even doubted the fine citizens of Truelove coming through in the end?"

They wandered out to the sidewalk to check on progress. "I want this to be the café Kara always dreamed of." Will placed the chalkboard placard near the curb.

Eager to make amends, Zach and some of the other off-duty firefighters used the engine ladder to attach the striped awning over the entrance.

Will and AnnaBeth stepped out of the way as her husband, Jonas, and several other men removed small, round tables from the back of a rented moving van and scattered them around the sidewalk. A troop of children positioned the rattan chairs around the café-style tables.

At the corner Lila was putting the finishing touches on a small mural she'd painted on the side of the building. Her fiancé, Sam, and tons of other volunteers had repaired and painted the interior walls the bright, cheery yellow color AnnaBeth had selected. Reflecting Kara's French bistro vibe.

Callie and Maggie scurried about draping red checkerboard tablecloths on the sidewalk tables.

"She's going to love this, AnnaBeth." He couldn't believe the transformation from storm-damaged diner to Parisian street café. "Thank you so much."

Hands on her hips, AnnaBeth smiled. "Thank my mom. If she hadn't hosted that Monet-inspired garden party last summer, there's no way we could've found these items so quickly to outfit the restaurant."

Will had never met AnnaBeth's mother, Victoria, but he'd gathered that like Glorieta, the well-to-do socialite was an honorary Truelove Double Name Club member. "Your mom just had them sitting in storage all this time?"

Several of the ROMEOs had spent a good portion of the day shuttling items from AnnaBeth's childhood home in Charlotte.

"If you knew her, you wouldn't even think to ask that question. Of course she did. She adores this kind of thing. You need something for an event? Pick a theme." AnnaBeth snapped her fingers. "She'll have exactly what you want and more in no time flat."

Thanks to Miss IdaLee putting the word out on the Truelove grapevine, lots of townspeople had shown up on short notice to help this project become a reality.

Leo had taken charge of putting the kitchen to rights. Shayla and Trudy swept up broken glass. Ethan reupholstered the booths. Bridger and Jake installed a new glass door, and the Allen clan oversaw the installation of the windows overlooking Main Street. GeorgeAnne had insisted on supplying the work team with all the needed supplies.

"Chef alert!" Paintbrush in hand, Lila poked her head around the corner of the lime-washed brick building. "Batten down the hatches, everyone. She's coming down the block, and she doesn't look too happy."

He straightened. Everyone sped up their pace in a rush to finish.

"The rest is up to you now." AnnaBeth patted his shoulder. "I'm going to head inside and make sure everything is ready for the final reveal."

He scrubbed his face with his hand.

"You got this. Just don't forget to tell her how you feel."

He prayed Kara would give him the chance to do that. Before she let him have it.

Will had one chance and one chance only. And he didn't mean to waste it.

Charging down the block, Kara slowed at the sight of the scaffolding erected next to the building. Her building. And was that Lila drawing an outline of the Eiffel Tower?

Juxtaposed against a Mason jar. Filled with what appeared to be sweet tea and a slice of lemon.

She craned her neck. "Lila?"

Peering down, her friend waved briefly, before she returned to painting in the letters that spelled out Mason Jar Café.

What was going on?

Picking up speed again, she rushed around the corner. The sight that met her eyes halted her in her tracks. Her mouth dropped open.

More than slightly discombobulated, her gaze pinged from Luke and Zach affixing a red-and-white-striped awning over the front entrance, over to the cheerful red-and-white geraniums ErmaJean and her granddaughters were planting in the moss-lined window boxes someone had erected.

The tables. The chairs. Her friends and customers bustled about. Except for Will, standing beside a blackboard placard, which read Welcome to the Mason Jar Café, Home of Truelove's Apple Galettes.

"What is going on here?"

"Everyone wanted to show you how important you and the café are to us."

She did a slow three-sixty. "I can't believe you did this... It's exactly how I envisioned the Mason Jar, but I didn't have the money to do this when I remodeled the restaurant. As an outsider, I was afraid of doing too much change too soon."

A muscle worked in his jaw. "You're not an outsider. Not anymore. And everyone is sorry we ever made you feel that way."

She went from table to table, thanking the volunteers, touching a flower petal, fingering the tablecloths. She couldn't quite believe this was real. That people had done this for her.

Taking her arm, he brought her inside and gave her the grand tour. Leo. Shayla. Trudy. Their commitment and loyalty meant so much. Sam was packing up paintbrushes and sealing up paint cans. Ethan gathered up his tools.

AnnaBeth hugged her. "We'll talk soon." Catching sight of one of the ROMEOs out on the sidewalk, her expression sharpened. The older man was a retired school administrator. "But right now there's someone I want Miss ErmaJean to meet."

On their way out the door, everyone wished Kara well and expressed their warm regards. Finally, only she and Will remained in the café.

"Is this what you imagined?" He looked at her. "We tried to get it right. Based on the journal you shared with AnnaBeth."

She was amazed and touched beyond words.

"It's perfect." Her lips quivered. "Better than I could've imagined. I love it."

"Your own little piece of Paris."

"Why did you do this for me, Will?" She ran her hand over the smooth, cool surface of the counter. "Why did everyone do this?"

"This is Truelove's expression of love for all you've done for our community. When faced with the prospect of losing you, everyone wanted to show how much you and your food mean to us. Something we realized almost too late." He swallowed. "We aren't too late, are we?"

"An expression of love?" she whispered.

"Everyone loves you, Kara."

She bit her lip. "Does that include you, too?"

"Me most of all." His gaze never left hers. "I went into panic mode when I heard the council's decision to close the firehouse. The sky felt like it was falling. I was wrong. And pigheaded. And stubborn. And stupid. And…" He folded his arms across his chest. "Feel free to stop me at any time."

She flicked her eyes at him. "Please, feel free to carry on. Get it out of your system once and for all."

"I'm never going to get you out of my system. And I never want to. I want you to know that if you choose to stay in Truelove, or if you choose to go, I support whatever you decide is best. I support you. Maddox and I just want to be wherever you are."

"But what about your job? Being a firefighter?"

"I love being a firefighter, but I don't love anything as much as I love you." His eyes bored into hers. "I lied to you that afternoon about not seeing a future for us. Worst of all, I was lying to myself."

She bit her lip. And he wanted to kiss her so bad. To take the pain from her eyes. Sorrow he'd caused. Had he crushed the love she felt for him? Was it too late?

But if he'd learned anything from Kara, he'd learned he must open his heart, show his heart, to have any chance at hers. To be worthy of her.

"I love you, Kara. I'll find another firehouse and commute if I have to, or find some other work. But the important thing is that we're together."

Tears sprang to her eyes.

"Forever." Taking her hand, he went down on one knee. "Because, darlin', when I look at you, I see the rest of my life."

She put her hand to her throat.

"I want to spend my life loving you. Will you marry me? Will you marry Maddox and me?"

Her mouth trembled. In his gaze, she beheld his heart. And his was a heart of love. For her. For her dreams.

"Yes," she whispered. "I love you so much, Will. Yes."

He took her in his arms. And in his embrace, she knew she'd found the forever home she'd been searching for her entire life.

"We should tell Maddox."

His fingers twined with hers, they moved out to the sidewalk. "Glorieta and Pops, too."

"Do you think he'll mind sharing his dad with me?"

Will squeezed her hand. "Are you kidding? The better

question is, will he share his Kara with dear old dad? That boy of mine is nuts about you."

She laughed. "What great taste he has."

Feigning surprise, he widened his gaze. "Hey, what about my taste?"

She patted his chest. "You are still a culinary work in progress."

"Chief!"

Letting go of each other, they angled as Mayor Watson, red-faced and puffing, lumbered toward them from the direction of the town hall.

"I'm so glad I caught you..." The mayor wheezed. "Big news." He placed his hands on his knees, struggling to regain his breath. "Big. Big. The biggest, greatest news." Beads of perspiration dotted the area around the white bandage on his forehead.

"Sir? Take it easy. Don't try to talk. Breathe in through your nostrils. And blow it out through your lips. Breathe in through—"

"The town council called an emergency meeting." The mayor's blue eyes gleamed. "And they reversed their earlier decision. Truelove will keep its fire station."

"But the budget?" Will shook his head. "I don't under—"

"The tornado yesterday provided some much-needed clarity to our more stubborn council members. Thanks to the valiant and heroic efforts of our own TFD, no lives were lost. It could've been so much worse, except for the quick action taken by the fire department. The necessary budget adjustments will be made, but no firefighter jobs will be lost."

She grasped his arm. "Oh, Will. How wonderful."

"My men will be so relieved." He extended his hand. "Thank you, Mayor. You championed the department throughout this entire ordeal. I fully appreciate all you've done to make this happen for my crew."

"When I said, no jobs lost—" the mayor shook his hand "—I meant no jobs lost, Will. I wouldn't blame you if you decided to look for greener pastures, but the council would like for you to stay on at the TFD, as well."

He swallowed.

The mayor gripped Will's shoulder. "Your leadership is invaluable to this town. I realize you may have already made plans to take a position at a bigger firehouse. To a bigger city that can offer you so much more than True-love ever could. After the way the council treated you, I wouldn't blame you. But would you give the town another chance to prove how much we appreciate your service?"

Will turned toward Kara. "What do you think?"

"I think if a certain French-loving chef is going to continue to run the Mason Jar, her favorite fire chief ought not to be too far away. God is good."

He faced the mayor. "Truelove has given me more than I could have ever asked for or imagined. Friends. Love. Home. There's no place I'd rather put down roots with my family. Thank you for the opportunity, Mayor."

"Thank you, Chief MacKenzie."

Will hugged Kara to his side as they watched the mayor head back toward the town hall. "Did that just happen?"

"Stick with me, Chief." Rising on her toes, she planted a kiss on his cheek. "The best is yet to be. Plus, free chocolate croissants at the station for life."

"Yep." He curled a strand of her hair around his index finger. "That's what I'm really counting on. Besides, if I didn't marry you first, I was afraid one of my firefighters would." He winked. "Those croissants of yours truly are quite something."

She play-smacked him. "You are so ridiculous."

"And you love me anyway?"

She looked down and then up at him. Leaving his heart lying in a puddle of melted jelly at his feet. "I'll love you always."

A sentiment that prompted him to kiss her again. No hard task there. And then she in turn felt compelled to return the gesture. Not that he was complaining.

She pulled back. "Enough of that for now. Take me to see my future son." She smiled. "Rain check?"

"I'm going to hold you to that."

She cocked her head. "I'll be looking forward to it."

He smiled. "Till then."

"Karwa!" Maddox shouted and ran down the block toward them.

Will frowned. "What's that he's carrying?"

She let go of his hand. "He's got something bundled in a jacket."

Will's navy blue TFD jacket.

Pops was doing his best to keep pace, but he lagged about two strides behind the little boy. "Will!"

His heart kicked up a notch. Both he and Kara raced forward. Maddox's face was red. As if he'd been crying.

Kara reached out her hand. "What's wrong? What's happened?"

Chest heaving, Pops caught up to them.

Amid the tears, Maddox's face shone. "Daddy! I found him. I found him."

There was a soft meow.

Her lips parted. "Maddox?" She started to shake. "Is that—? Is that…?"

Maddox folded back a corner of his jacket. A cream-colored cat poked out his head.

"Soufflé?" She reached for the little tabby. The cat leaped into her arms. She pressed her face against his fur.

"Oh, kitty cat. Where have you been? I've been so worried."

Eyes half-closed, ears forward, the tabby lay content in her arms and purred.

Pops grinned. "That is one happy cat."

Using the tip of his finger, Maddox stroked Soufflé's back. "I'm a weal firefighter, Daddy. I wescued Soufflé. I find him for you, Miss Karwa."

She sat down on the curb and pulled Maddox into her lap alongside the cat. "Thank you, Maddox." She kissed his forehead. "Thank you for finding Soufflé, sweet boy."

Will looked at his father. "How? Where?"

Pops grinned. "Maddox insisted Glorieta and I let him search the area around Kara's house again."

"But Kara and I both searched. There was no sign of him. Was he trapped under something?"

"We found him sitting on what was left of the back porch. Like he was just waiting for his people to show up." Pops scratched his head. "Best I can figure, when the tornado hit the house, maybe something fell onto the cage. The door must've popped open. And somehow Soufflé escaped through a broken window, or a crack in the wall before the entire house collapsed."

"But where has he been the last twenty-four hours?"

Pops shrugged. "We'll probably never know all the adventures he's seen. I'm just so happy he's okay." His dark eyes flickered. "If y'all will excuse me, I left Glorieta in our kitchen. She insisted on putting together a pre-Easter dinner. Deviled eggs, ham and biscuits were mentioned."

"And sweet tea?"

His father smiled. "Of course."

"We won't be far behind you, Dad."

"Good." Pops winked. "You know how testy these professional chefs get if you keep them waiting and their food gets cold." Whistling, hands in his pockets, he set off across the square toward home.

Maddox tucked his head under Kara's chin. "Soufflé wost his way home, but I help him find it. Now he never be wost again from his twue family."

She looked up at Will.

He sat down beside her, putting his arm around her, his son and the little cat. "Me, too. Lost nevermore. Not now that I've found my one true home and family." His voice hitched. "No more strays."

She touched Maddox's cheek. "Sweetie pie, what would you think about me coming to live at your house?"

He perked. "And be our cooker?"

Will bit back a smile. "Not exactly."

"I was thinking maybe you could be my little boy." A line puckered the space between her eyebrows. "And I could be your mommy." She moistened her bottom lip. "Would that be okay with you, Maddox?"

The child's features lit. "I dink dat would be de greatest idea ever." He flung one arm around Kara and the other around Will. "Now you won't be sad anymore."

"No," Will rasped. "I won't be sad anymore."

Maddox pulled the both of them close. "And I won't ever go hungwy for a mommy ever again."

"I love you so much, Maddox."

Will's eyes watered. Kara loving his son was such a beautiful, longed-for sight. She was the mommy Maddox had always been meant to have. And now they'd found each other.

"I wuv you." Maddox patted the tabby's small head. "And I wuv you, too, Soufflé." The cat purred.

Will rose and held out his hand. "Thank you for loving Maddox. Thank you for loving me."

She got to her feet. Soufflé jumped out of her arms to

the pavement. The cat rubbed his head against Kara's leg and then pranced forward.

"Wait for me, Soufflé." Maddox tugged at her hand. "Wait at de corner for me and Karwa and Daddy."

The fire chief kissed Kara's cheek. "And one day, I promise, I'll give you Paris."

Folding the jacket over her arm like a maître d', her eyes flitted to the Eiffel Tower painted on the wall.

"You already have." One hand on Maddox's head, she wrapped her arm around Will's waist. "And so much more."

* * * * *

If you enjoyed this story,
check out these other Truelove stories
from author Lisa Carter

His Secret Daughter
The Twin Bargain
Stranded for the Holidays
A Mother's Homecoming
The Christmas Bargain

Find these and other great reads at
www.LoveInspired.com

Dear Reader,

For me, change has never been easy. In this story, it seems as if everyone in Truelove is undergoing a season of change. Do you struggle with change? On their journey of faith, Kara and Will must let go of the past if they hope to truly embrace the beautiful future God has planned for them.

A tornado wreaks destruction on Truelove, but provides an opportunity for its citizens to choose love and forgiveness. This is the spiritual truth I'm learning right now—that every day, in every situation, with every relationship—we are given the choice to choose love and forgiveness. Or not.

Oftentimes living within the contexts of our life relationships we find it challenging to live in peace with each other, with ourselves and with God. And yet, we must not only choose to love our neighbors, but to also show our love in practical, visible actions.

Like Soufflé, once upon a time you and I were strays until God made a way for us to become part of His family. Jesus Christ's sacrifice is the ultimate expression of love. And it is through Him, we find our forever Home—the true Happily-Ever-After for which we were created.

I hope you enjoyed taking this journey with Kara, Will, Maddox and little Soufflé. I would love to hear from you. Email me at lisa@lisacarterauthor.com or visit www.lisacarterauthor.com.

In His Love,
Lisa Carter

WE HOPE YOU ENJOYED
THIS BOOK FROM

LOVE INSPIRED
INSPIRATIONAL ROMANCE

Uplifting stories of faith, forgiveness and hope.

Fall in love with stories where faith helps
guide you through life's challenges, and discover
the promise of a new beginning.

6 NEW BOOKS AVAILABLE EVERY MONTH!

COMING NEXT MONTH FROM
Love Inspired

AN AMISH MOTHER FOR HIS TWINS
North Country Amish • by Patricia Davids
Amish widow Maisie Schrock is determined to help raise her late sister's newborn twins, but first she must convince her brother-in-law that she's the best person for the job. Nathan Weaver was devastated when his wife deserted him, but can he trust her identical sister with his children...and his heart?

THEIR SURPRISE AMISH MARRIAGE
by Jocelyn McClay
The last thing Rachel Mast expected was to end up pregnant and married—to her longtime beau's brother. But with her ex abruptly gone from the Amish community, can Rachel and Benjamin Raber build their marriage of convenience into a forever love?

THE MARINE'S MISSION
Rocky Mountain Family • by Deb Kastner
While ex-marine Aaron Jamison always follows orders, an assignment to receive a service dog and evaluate the company isn't his favorite mission—especially when trainer Ruby Winslow insists on giving him a poodle. But training with Ruby and the pup might be just what he needs to get his life back on track...

HER HIDDEN LEGACY
Double R Legacy • by Danica Favorite
To save her magazine, RaeLynn McCoy must write a story about Double R Ranch—and face the estranged family she's never met. But when ranch foreman Hunter Hawkins asks for help caring for the nieces and nephew temporarily in his custody, her plan to do her job and leave without forming attachments becomes impossible...

THE FATHER HE DESERVES
by Lisa Jordan
Returning home, Evan Holland's ready to make amends and heal. But when he discovers Natalie Bishop—the person he hurt most by leaving—has kept a secret all these years, he's not the only one who needs forgiveness. Can he and Natalie reunite to form a family for the son he never knew existed?

A DREAM OF FAMILY
by Jill Weatherholt
All Molly Morgan ever wanted was a family, but after getting left at the altar, she never thought it would happen—until she's selected to adopt little Grace. With her business failing, her dream could still fall through...unless businessman Derek McKinney can help turn her bookstore around in time to give Grace a home.

LICNM0621

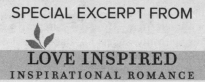
"Oscar will be perfect for your needs," Ruby assured Aaron,
reaching down to scratch the poodle's head.

"That froufrou dog? No way, ma'am. Not gonna happen."

"Excuse me?" She'd expected him to hesitate but not
downright reject her idea.

"Look, Ruby, if you like Oscar so much, then keep him
for yourself. I need a man's dog by my side, not some…
some…"

"Poodle?" Ruby suggested, her eyebrows disappearing
beneath her long ginger bangs.

"Right. Lead me to where you keep the German
shepherds, and I'll pick one out myself."

"Hmm," Ruby said, rubbing her chin as if considering his
request, although she really wasn't. "No."

"No?"

"No," she repeated firmly. "First off, we don't currently
have a German shepherd as part of our program."

"I'd even take a pit bull." He was beginning to sound
desperate.

"Look, Aaron. Either you're going to have to learn to
trust me or you may as well just leave now before we start.
This isn't going to work unless you're ready to listen to me
and do whatever I tell you to do."

His eyebrows furrowed. "I understand chain of command, ma'am. There were many times as a marine when I didn't exactly agree with my superiors, but I understood why it was important to follow orders."

"Okay. Let's go with that."

"For me," Aaron continued, "following orders is black-and-white. My marines' lives under my command often depended on it. But as you can see, I'm having difficulty making that transition in this situation. We're not talking people's lives here."

"I disagree. We're very much talking lives—*yours*. You may not yet have a clear vision of what you'll be able to do with Oscar, but a service dog can make all the difference."

"Yes, but you just insisted the best dog for me is a *poodle*. I'm sorry, but if you knew anything about me at all, you'd know the last dog in the world I'd choose would be a poodle."

"And yet I still believe I'm right," said Ruby with a wry smile. Somehow, she had to convince this man she knew what she was doing. "I carefully studied your file before you arrived, Aaron, and specially selected Oscar for you to work with. I'm the expert here. So how are we going to get over this hurdle?"

"I have orders to make this work. How will it look if I give up before I even start the process?" He shook his head. "No. Don't answer that. It will look as if I wasn't able to complete my mission. That's never going to happen. I'll *always* pull through, no matter what."

Don't miss
The Marine's Mission *by Deb Kastner,*
available July 2021 wherever
Love Inspired books and ebooks are sold.

LoveInspired.com

IF YOU ENJOYED THIS BOOK, DON'T MISS NEW EXTENDED-LENGTH NOVELS FROM LOVE INSPIRED!

In addition to the Love Inspired books you know and love, we're excited to introduce even more uplifting stories in a longer format, with more inspiring fresh starts and page-turning thrills!

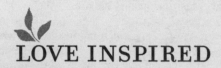

LOVE INSPIRED

Stories to uplift and inspire.

Fall in love with stories of faith, forgiveness and hope. Be inspired by characters overcoming life's challenges, and the promise of new beginnings.

LOOK FOR THESE LOVE INSPIRED TITLES ONLINE AND IN THE BOOK DEPARTMENT OF YOUR FAVORITE RETAILER!

LITRADE0621